CW00428809

The Journalists

Congo Rescue

By

Mark Gadsdon

The Journalists - Congo Rescue

markgadsdon@yahoo.co.uk

The Journalists - Congo Rescue

Also by Mark Gadsdon

Adventure /Romance
Three Nights in Bangkok

Action Adventure /Romance
The Journalists - A Rose Among Thones

Thrillers
Bangkok Heroes
Bangkok Heroes 11

Children's Books
Nathan's Friends The Missing Girls
Nathan's Friends The Secret Room
Nathan's Friend's The School Ghosts

To come
The Journalists -

The Journalists - Congo Rescue

Prologue
Chapter One
Chapter Two
Chapter Three
Chapter Four
Chapter Five
Chapter Six
Chapter Seven
Chapter Eight
Chapter Nine
Chapter Ten
Chapter Eleven
ChapterTwelve
Chapter Thirteen
Chapter fourteen
Chapter fifteen
Chapter Sixteen
Chapter Seventeen
Chapter Eighteen
Chapter Nineteen
Chapter Twenty
Chapter Twenty One
Chapter Twenty Two
Chapter Twenty Three
Chapter Twenty Four
Chapter Twenty Five
Chapter Twenty Six

Prologue

2003: Democratic Republic of Congo. (DRC)

A month had passed since a peace agreement had been signed to end a civil war that was known as the second Congo war and by some referred to as the African world war. It had been a war that had dragged nine other African countries into its web of violence and destruction, killing more than five million people. Various rebel groups, twenty-five it's said, had ravaged the country, all looking for a piece or a place in power until a testimonial government had taken power. Meanwhile, more than five million people had died, if not by a bullet or a savage beaten, by disease or starvation. For the younger generation of the Congolese people it was all they knew. Civil war after civil war, massacre after massacre, innocent civilians lined up and shot like cattle, before the rebel groups would go to the next village and do the same, just because their warlords had ordered it.

Even now, a month after the peace agreement had been signed, more than a thousand people a day were dying at the hands of certain rebel groups who weren't in favour of the so called government, a government who'd offered them nothing. The most prominent of these was a group three thousand men strong and lead by a ruthless Warlord by the name of Joseph Kabila. Various officials in various African countries, whom Kamila was taking his instructions, had insisted he kept his men in the DRC. It was a DRC civil war and they didn't want it spreading over the borders. He'd crossed the Zaire, river and massacred an entire village in the republic of Congo. It had been decided by all nine African country's that were involved in the war that, he couldn't be trusted, he was too violent. Those who dared, even suggested he was insane.

--Chapter One--

HOT, HUMID AND bloody uncomfortable was how John Stone was describing the climate while he sat at a bar after ordering a Johnnie Walker and soda. He sat there wondering what gorillas urine would smell like, partly because he knew there were gorillas in the Congo-Basin, and partly because he was sure it would resemble the so called whisky he was drinking.

Stale with a certain whiff to it, that was not even close to the smell of a good whisky. Before John had even ordered it he knew it wasn't going to be Johnnie Walker, but had wished it was going to smell and taste a little better than it did. He knew it was probably brewed in the bar owners back yard or supplied by someone who'd done the same, in his back yard, in conditions that for sure didn't meet with international hygiene standards. But as stale as it was and even with the awful smell that seem to linger in the bar as he drank it, he did appreciate the fact it had some kick to it, because that was all he was looking for.

His assignment was to report on the Aids pandemic that was spreading across Africa like a plague of locust might spread across a harvest. He'd just come from Kinshasa's general hospital. What he'd seen was not for the weak, faint hearted or feeble minded. Even he had struggled to console himself, and he'd thought there was nothing that could bother him now, not after all he'd seen.

While he'd passed through the wards of the poorly equipped hospital, he'd seen people lying on excrement soaked beds, their bodies eaten away by the virus, leaving nothing but skin and bones, both young and old dying slowly and painfully in the care of nurses, that wanted, but had no clue how to ease their suffering.

He sat at the open bar with his back facing the road while listening to the traffic that passed by behind him. He then took another large sip of the whisky that wasn't actually whiskey, as he shook his head in disbelief. He'd seen some dreadful things during his career as a Journalist and more so while he was in the forces, but most were the consequences of war, or people who had just massacred a village and deserved to die. But this was different, these were not bad people, or ruthless rebels. These were just innocent civilians, innocent mothers and fathers, just going about their lives taking care of their children who now sat beside them, watching them die.

The agency he worked for had, for the very first time given him an option, this assignment or going to Somalia to report on a western family that had been murdered while staying at a holiday resort in Mogadishu. He knew the reason for this was because they thought this assignment might be more than even he could endure. He now wished he'd chosen the latter, even though he knew Somalia was one of the most dangerous countries in the world.

'Give us another one, Nelson,' John asked, while tapping his glass on the wooden bar, and looking at his friend.

'One more it is, no ice, right, John.'

'That's right, Nelson,' John insisted. He knew adding ice might be a risk to far. As it was, he knew the hangover he was for sure going to have would be bad enough, especially after drinking what he was drinking, but typhoid was rife here and it was through drinking dirty water. He understood these people had to make a living somehow, and knew these people couldn't afford to sell the real thing. The only people who could afford to drink Johnnie Walker here, which was actually three times as expensive as it was in Scotland or England, were the officials.

John, of course, could, afford to buy it, but the only places that sold it were the more expensive hotels, which as far as John was concerned weren't worth the money they expected you to pay.

This wasn't John's first visit to Kinshasa nor was it his first time in this bar, hence the reason he knew Nelson who had owned the bar for some time now. John swiveled around on his bar stool and faced the main street. He wasn't so surprised to see everyone getting on with their lives, despite just having ended a civil war that had killed millions of people, to be faced with a virus that could easily kill just as many. He knew that anyone younger than twenty-five would have seen nothing else other than death and destruction, and that there'd hardly be a family left that hadn't had a member of it killed by a rebel or government soldier.

The Journalists - Congo Rescue

It was depressing just thinking about it and he was glad his job here was coming to an end. He smiled to himself knowing there was just one more place to visit, though the smile left his face just as quick knowing where that place was. Goma was often referred to as being the most dangerous city in the world, for the people that lived there in any case. Not only because it is located in the midst of a war zone where civilians were routinely slaughtered or raped by soldiers or rebels, but it was also threatened by a volcano that overlooked the small city, just waiting to spew its red hot lather over its residents.

He could take some reprieve in knowing that the war had just ended, but was sure there'd still be rebel groups doing what they did best.

He continued to watch the Congolese people going about their lives with a feeling of compassion, knowing for sure that their lives had been hard, harder than any western person could probably endure.

The aroma in the area that encircled the bar was not pleasant. A cattle market was positioned just across the road, where cows and goats would be slaughtered out in the open, while the buyer stood waiting for his leg of beef, or a whole goat after it had had its throat slit before being skinned. Just at the back of the bar was a fish market where John knew the Congo River passed, the second longest river in the world that would snake its way through the Congo Basin. Here fish would be gutted and filleted if not sold whole. Any waste, that would be only the guts, would be thrown back into the river. The wooden tables used to fillet the fish on, were ingrained with previous fish guts that even the millions of flies hadn't managed to consume.

This was an area on the outskirts of Kinshasa, in a place called Gare Centrale which was northern Kinshasa and would be easy to pick up the n1 highway that would take John to Goma, and was the main reason he was staying there.

There weren't many westerners that travelled to this part of Kinshasa, or stayed at any of its cheap hotels, in fact, John couldn't remember seeing any, at least not until now. Now he was staring at a face across the street that was watching while a local cut the throat of a goat. It was a face that had a hand over its mouth, while with a look of degust. It was a face that was for sure western but not European, South American, John considered. A face that was tanned a golden brown, a pretty face, a beautiful face. She looked like a female Indiana Jones wearing a khaki, coloured shirt and shorts that seem to enhance the colour of her long thin, but strong looking legs. She wore a large, almost cowboy style hat, and hiker boots that looked as though they hadn't even seen dirt. She also had a small shoulder bag that was resting on her hip, and was also Khaki though a slightly darker shade.

John turned his head when he saw she turned her head, not wanting her to see him staring, and he was staring. He'd never seen such an attractive woman, at least not here. He swung back around on his stool and faced the bar, while wanting to swing back around and watch her. Picking up his glass he caught a glance of her in the reflection, it wasn't a clear reflection from the well used glass, but it was clear enough to see she was heading right for him. He continued to sip his drink as though he hadn't even seen her. He could smell her perfume just as she had approached, even through the awful smell that lingered.

'Good afternoon,' she said, looking at John while moving up close, very close. 'Good match don't you think,' she said with a smile that showed off her perfect gleaming white teeth.

John was surprised and just wanted to put his arm around her and give her a kiss, but as he looked down he could see she was just referring to the colour of their trousers, both being khaki. 'Ah, yes,

I see what you mean, a perfect match at that,' he said after thinking she was referring to him and her.

'Can I buy you another drink,' she asked with a small flicker of her eyes and after she had taken a step back.

John would have preferred it if she hadn't taken a step back. 'Oh, right, well, okay, I'll have a small bottle of water then, please.'

'Oh, are you sure, I'm happy to buy you whatever it is you're drinking. What is that anyhow?' she asked, looking at the murky water like substance in his glass.

While smiling John lifted his glass and placed it just under her nose.

Her eyes opened wide and her head whipped back before saying. 'Oh gosh!' She placed her hand between John's drink and her nose. 'I think two small bottles of water will do, just fine,' she said, now waving her hand at John's glass as if trying to extinguish the smell.

'Nelson, two small bottles of water, please.'

'I'm Martina Gomez,' she said, holding a hand out.

'John Stone,' John said, unavoidably noticing her small but stunning Patok Philippe watch, and the white band on her centre finger where he guessed she would have normally worn an expensive ring, judging by the watch.

Nelson placed their water on the bar in front of them after retrieving it from a large ice container. 'Glasses?'

'No, not for me,' John insisted.

'Yes, thank you,' Martina said, while removing the top to her bottle and placing her small backside on a bar stool that sat next to John's.

John didn't want to start the conversation with the question he was about to ask, but just had to know. 'So, what's a girl like you doing in a place like this?'

Martina laughed out loud, but not too loud. 'Well, I guess that's a fair question,' she said, while wondering about the same of him. *What's a handsome man like him doing in a place like this?'* 'I'm here to visit the gorillas.'

John sat quiet for a second not sure if she was joking or not. 'Are you mad,' he said, after realising she was being completely serious.

'No, I'm here to see the gorillas, why is that mad, I've always wanted to see the gorillas,' she shrugged her shoulders, taken aback a little at John's words, and with him looking as though he thought she was actually mad.

'Alone?' John asked, with a look of shock, while looking at a girl who he knew had never been to a place like this and probably had no idea of the dangers.

'No, of course not alone, there's a team of us,' she said now realising he was just being considerate.

John wiped his brow while smiling. 'Phew, okay then.'

'Oh, John, now I know why you were looking at me as though you thought I was a little crazy.'

John nodded. He wanted to ask what kind of team and how big a team it was. He also wanted to ask if they'd be armed or if they even had a local guide to take them, but he knew it really was none of his business and thought it better not to get involved, which he knew he easily could as he watched Martina sip her water.

'John you haven't told me what a man like you is doing in a place like this,' Martina said, smiling, then getting another small whiff of his drink as the aroma passed under her nose. 'John, how can you drink that?'

'Ah, well, the thing is I'm a journalist, and I'm here to report on the Aids Pandemic and how bad it is here. . .'

'Isn't it terrible,' Martina interrupts.

The Journalists - Congo Rescue

'Yes, it is, but I didn't realise just how terrible until I visited the hospital only this morning.'

'Oh my god, that must have been horrible, John.'

'It was, hence the drink,' John said, raising his glass.

Martina was enjoying talking to John and was finding him quite appealing, but that wasn't why she'd approached him. She was looking for someone to take her and her team up north. She knew it had to be someone who knew the jungle and knew how to survive in the jungle. She needed someone who could handle weapons, someone who could protect them if needed. She was sure John wasn't that man, he's just a journalist after all, but that didn't mean she couldn't continue to get to know him. She liked the way he'd combed his hair back and the way it suited his handsome looks. His tanned skin almost matching hers, and his stubble she found particularly appealing. She looked into his blue eyes. 'So, am I right in thinking you're from the UK, John?'

John was impressed at how well she spoke English, and was enjoying just sitting there speaking to her. Not only was she beautiful with beautiful brown eyes that he couldn't avoid staring into. She also seemed well mannered and polite.

'Yes, London as it happens, have you been to the UK?'

'No, I haven't, but I hope to go there someday.'

'You should, I'm sure you'd enjoy it, so, I'm guessing you're from South America, what with the accent and the tanned skin,' John said, looking down at her legs as she sat on the stool, and wanting to run his hands along her smooth skin.

'Yes, you guessed right, John, I'm from Rio, Brazil. Have you been there?' She guessed he might have. She could see he was a well travelled man, and being a Journalist and all.

'No, my agency doesn't send me to places like that.' John wanted to tell her why but decided against it. 'They normally send me to places like this.' John shrugged.

'Well, don't beat yourself up about not going to Brazil, I mean it is a beautiful country and I love it of course, but the crime rate there is probably no better than this place, you can't walk alone in Rio, not at night anyhow.'

John knew what she was saying was true, the crime rate was high, and he knew walking the streets of Rio at night, alone, whether you were male or female would without doubt result in you getting mugged, or worse. He also knew you couldn't compare Rio, or anywhere in Brazil to this place. But he wasn't about to get into that conversation, which he knew he could rant on about for the rest of the day and still not finish talking about the atrocities that had been carried out here, and just to gain a little power. 'Um, I know the crime rate is high there, it's such a shame because it's such a beautiful place, as you say.'

'Yes, it really is, John,' she said, obviously saddened at John's words.

'So, what is it you do, Martina?' John asked, not wanting the conversation to end, and just realising he hadn't thought about this morning's experience at the general hospital since she'd sat down beside him.

'I'm a jeweller; actually it's my father's business. Martina shrugged. 'It's all I know, I've been doing it since I left school.'

'Wow, you mean cutting the jewels and all that?'

'Yes, cutting the diamonds, rubies, whatever, and designing the gold mounts too, whether it's a ring bracelet or necklace.'

'Wow that's quite a skill, Martina.'

'Yes, it is, John,' she said nodding.

'Well, well done, you.'

'Thank you, John,' Martina said, with a smile of appreciation.

For the next hour they'd laughed and joked. John had told her things about him that normally he would have only shared with his closest family members. The same could be said about Martina, and she had even told John what kind of man she liked, while describing a man that had mirrored him perfectly, though John wasn't sure whether she actually realised that.

Then, suddenly, she looked the other way. 'I have to go, my father's waiting,' she then hesitated before saying. 'Well, it's been a pleasure, John.'

John could see a man who he assumed must be her father waiting across the road, a quite good looking man for his age with a neatly trimmed almost white beard. 'You too Martina, you take care out in the jungle, hey.'

'I will John, thank you,' she said, while not wanting to leave and looking into John's eyes that she knew she might not see again.

One minute she was there and the next she was disappearing down the street. Happy one minute, and feeling depressed the next. John had really enjoyed the short time he'd spent with Martina, a woman he'd guessed was about twenty-eight possibly thirty. A woman he now wished he'd asked if she'd had a local guide to take them into the jungle. He'd also wanted to ask her what kind of team she was speaking about and if they were experienced trackers, and knew the jungle and all the dangers he felt sure they would encounter. He now, with concern flowing through his veins, wished he had.

'Nice looking woman, John,' Nelson said, resting his elbows on the bar where John was sitting, and watching her petite backside sway slightly as she walked.

'Yes, Nelson, very nice looking indeed.' John agreed, while wishing she hadn't had to go so quickly.

--Chapter Two--

THE JUNGLE WAS dense, the tall trees reaching up into the canopy like arms with the fingers spread. Birds and chimpanzees could be heard singing up above. The natural vegetation was thick and barely passable, where snakes would sliver in search of their next meal. Because of the natural canopy that blocked out the sun, it was dark. The hot boggy earth of the swamp had released a mist, making it murky and creepy. Voices could be heard, they were getting closer. 'Who, is that?' Martina asked, petrified, terrified. Suddenly, they were surrounded by rebels wielding their machetes, waving them in the air. Their faces were mean and aggressive, their bodies scarred all over. 'Are they going to kill us, John?' John couldn't move, he wanted to help but the vegetation wrapped itself around him as he tried. The rebels approached Martina, swamping her small figure, looking down at her, watching her shake.

'Martina!' John shouted.

The rebels raised their machetes high, about to slice Martina into pieces.

'Martina!' John shouted again.

He was too late; there was nothing he could do.

The rebels brought down their machetes with such force.

'Martina! Martina!'

John suddenly woke up in a cold sweat that dripped from his brow and ran down his face. His shirt was drenched and his hands were clammy. 'Holly shit,' he said to himself, wiping his brow, after realising it was all just a dream.

It had been late afternoon by the time he'd made his way back to the hotel, and as he often did, had decided to take an afternoon nap.

He wiped his brow again before retrieving a small bottle of water from the small fridge. He then undid the lid before he gulped it down in one, while pieces of the dream he'd had flickered in his mind. It hadn't been a nice dream and he had no clue as to why he'd had it other than feeling a little guilty. He was now wishing he'd made sure that Martina was properly prepared to go into the jungle, which he felt sure she wasn't.

Though there was one thing he was grateful for, and that was that he didn't have a hangover. He put it down to Martina turning up and then drinking water rather than the disgusting drink he otherwise would have drunk plenty of.

After sitting there a while just looking around his room at the smoke stained walls and the paint peeling off the ceiling. He grabbed a towel from the bottom of the bed and headed to the shower room. Once in the shower room he stripped down and threw his closes out through the door. The shower was not great, barely warm, with inconsistent spurts that seem to catch him in the eye each time he looked up to try and improve the flow by wiping the shower head with his hand. After he'd washed his hair he just stood there for a while, letting the water run over his head and down his body. He started to think about the poor souls he'd visited that morning. He knew it was something that would remain with him for a while at least. He also knew that trying to block it from his mind would be futile, but John had his ways of handling things like this, and it wasn't by blocking it out of his mind. He'd focus his mind on what he had seen, and remain focused for some time. He knew, at least for him, the best way to cope was to face it. He'd done the same while he was in the Special Forces and also when he was in the paratroopers. During his career, he'd seen things that no man should ever see. Bodies dismembered by large calibre machine guns, men without their legs after standing on a mine, and men that had been decapitated my Islamic insurgents. It never completely helped, but just focusing on it rather than trying not to think about it - helped a little.

John's hair fell back into position like a well trained soldier as he combed it back effortlessly. He'd always done it like this even when he was just a lad, and now it was as though it knew, and was pleased to oblige. He admired himself in the mirror while he brushed his teeth, though unlike like most men, he didn't particularly like what he saw. John was now in his mid thirties and the small lines around his eyes highlighted by his tanned skin had reminded him of that. The last fifteen years of his life were exhilarating, but hard. And it was now starting to show. He'd seen and done things no man should have to see or do. But all said and done, it was the life he felt was meant for him. Sitting at home in his slippers watching TV with a cup of tea in his hand, just wasn't him.

There had been times when he had wondered what he was doing with his life, and why he hadn't settled down, but those days had disappeared like Martina had only that afternoon. He knew it was just a brief meeting and was sure after a few days she will vanish from his mind like so many had before, but for now at least, her beautiful brown eyes were as clear as day and it was as though he still sat beside her at the bar.

His armpits were cool after giving them a couple of squirts of his favourite deodorant, before putting on his Khaki coloured shirt which had large pockets where he placed his cigarettes and lighter. It was early evening and he hadn't had a thing to eat all day, so now he was looking forward to visiting the small café that he knew was on the ground floor. With one last glance around his room to make sure he hadn't forgotten anything, he grabbed the key and left.

The café was small with African ornaments that were scattered all around, and African style pictures that filled the walls. It was small but cosy and John knew they had a western menu, if you didn't feel the need to try out some of the African meals. He'd found himself a table next to the window, which wasn't hard as he was the only one in there. He knew it was because he was early, and was sure it would pick up as the evening went on. It always did, and he was sure it was because the service was always good, and very professional, and the reason for this was now approaching him dressed in his chef's outfit.

'Welcome back, John, I wasn't expecting to see you here again so soon. Not after what happened the last time you were here. I do hope you are trying to avoid clashing into him again.'

'Thank you Benjamin, actually I hadn't given him a thought. Has he been back to harass your staff again?'

'No, actually, I haven't seen him since that night. You really showed them John, are you sure you're just a journalist. I mean you went through him and his men like they weren't even there.'

The last time John had been posted to the Congo and stayed at this hotel he'd witnessed Bamboula, a local bully apparently, and his men harassing Benjamin's staff. He'd taken it upon himself to teach him and his men a lesson in good manners. He hadn't wanted to, the last thing he needed was to bring attention to himself in a place like this, but just watching them pick on the young staff at the hotel was a little more than he was prepared to stand. Bamboula had had three men with him, and since John had intervened, he had learned they were a constant headache for the locals as well as the hotel staff. John knew he'd recognise him immediately if he was to run into him again, because he'd have a scar on the left side if his face, something John had given him as a reminder. 'No, I'm just a journalist Benjamin, though I have taking a few lessons in self defense.'

'Well, good on you, John,' Benjamin said, with a smile full of appreciation. 'So, what are you having to eat, you know you really should try some of the African meals, I promise there aren't any fruit-bats on the menu,' he said, laughing.

John was never an adventurous eater and much preferred to stick to things he recognised, and he also knew that fruit-bats where the cause of the last outbreak of Ebola that had killed thousands of people in Africa before it was contained. But he appreciated Benjamin's sense of humour, and knew if he was going to be doing the cooking it would be fine. 'Okay, Benjamin, I'll leave it up to you, but make sure it's well cooked, won't you.'

'Of course, John.' He then clapped his hands, bringing all his staff out from where they'd been. They set John's table as if it was the Savoy, and not some small café in a cheap hotel. He knew it was all just to show their appreciation for him getting rid of a bully that had been pestering them for some time, but didn't feel it was necessary to go to such extremes.

'Compliments of the house, sir,' a young Congolese man said with a smile so wide. He was holding a bottle in his hand, a bottle that John had recognised instantly. He poured a single measure of the Johnnie Walker into a whiskey glass before saying. 'What would you like with it, sir?'

John smiled while becoming quite emotional. 'Soda will do nicely, thank you.'

He sat drinking his whiskey, which he knew for sure was the real thing, while glancing at a menu that stood at the top of the table and was in a small holder that contained two small glass salt and pepper pots. At the top of the menu clearly printed was the name of the hotel - the Welcome Hotel. As he continued to drink his whiskey he couldn't deny it, it was indeed a welcoming hotel.

It was some thirty minutes before his meal was finally served, but seemed a lot less now he was on his third whiskey. A large bowl of rice was placed on the table by his good friend Benjamin, who was actually the head chef and wouldn't normally be serving in the café, which to John now felt like a posh restaurant. After the rice came some kind of meat dish, though John had no idea what it was. Finally came the vegetables which were steaming and misting up the window a little.

'Wow!' John said, looking at a meal he was sure even the officials would be lucky to have been served.

'Enjoy your meal, John,' Benjamin said, looking proud as punch.

John was sure he would as the aroma coming from the meat dish passed under his nose. After he'd served himself with some rice and vegetables, and adding them to the meat dish, he was sure the meat was lamb and tasted delightful.

It was some moments later when the small café started to fill, but John was too busy enjoying his meal to notice. Even to busy it seemed to notice the group of five westerners that had walked straight by him and made their way to the back of the café.

The staff was keeping a close eye on John and waiting on his every need. Most of the staff there were the ones that had been bullied and was now glad to be able to show their gratitude. John had just finished his main course with a wipe of his mouth using one of the napkins given to him, and that lay on his table. Before he'd even put the napkin down they'd cleared his table and brought him the sweets display that they'd wheeled from the other side of the café.

'Wow,' John expressed again, as he saw the choice he had. He felt sure he knew why the young waiters were paying him so much attention, and wanted to tell them there was really no need, but at the same time he could see all the trouble they'd gone to and didn't want to disappoint them. He scanned the sweets briefly, but it didn't take much before he'd glanced upon his favourite. 'I'll have the cheesecake with black-currant topping.'

Martina watched with curiosity flowing through her veins as John was being treated like a king. The rest of her team hadn't noticed, but she had as she continued to watch the young waiters deliver his coffee and biscuits after he'd finished his sweet. She'd seen it was only him and that no one else were getting such treatment. She'd seen how nice John was while talking to him at the bar, but she was sure that wasn't the reason he was being treated with such care and attention.

She wanted to go sit with him and continue the conversation that she had enjoyed so much that afternoon, not only so she could ask why he was being treated in such a professional manner, but mainly because he looked so handsome. She'd warmed to him that afternoon, but now as she looked on she felt herself wanting to be near him.

The team consisted of her father, his brother, and two close friends of her father who made it impossible for her to just leave the table to go sit with John, but she wanted to, oh how she wanted to.

John rubbed his stomach after he'd consumed his last biscuit, and finished his coffee. He felt satisfied, and full to the brim, he also knew if they were going to bring him anything else he would have to politely refuse.

Then, Benjamin appeared at his table again. 'Was everything to your liking, John?'

'Absolutely Benjamin, absolutely perfect,' John said, with a satisfying look on his face that had put a smile on Benjamin's face.

'So, what now John, have you finished your report yet,' Benjamin asked with a shrug.

'No, not quite, I have to go to Goma tomorrow, there's a small hospital there I have to visit.'

'Well, you take care, John, I'm sure you don't need me to tell you how dangerous that place is.'

'No, I'm well aware that Goma's a dangerous place, but it should be a little better now, right, what with the war ending I mean, or are there still rebel groups doing what they do best,' John asked, though suddenly for no reason felt sure he knew the answer.

'There is one, John, led by Joseph Kabila, he's a savage warlord. I believe he keeps himself hid deep in the jungle, but his men have been reported causing mayhem in Goma. I'd stay well clear if you come across them because they number in their thousands. I don't know why they insist on behaving like they do, I guess some people just don't like peace,' Benjamin said, with a shrug.

'Its power, Benjamin. Once they've had a taste of it, they don't want to let it go. People like them thrive on peoples fear, it's like a drug and they can't get enough of it, but don't worry about me, once I'm done there I'll be heading straight back here, and then to the UK.'

Benjamin was glad to hear that. He knew John could handle himself because he'd seen it first hand, but he also knew John would be no match for the rebel group he'd mentioned and sincerely hoped he'd be okay. 'Well, you're always welcome, John, oh, by the way, you can keep the bottle, take it back to your room you might feel like a little nightcap.'

'Thank you, Benjamin, and thank you for such a delightful meal.'

'You're more than welcome, John,' Benjamin said, before disappearing back into the kitchen.

The Journalists - Congo Rescue

John continued sitting there for a while, digesting his meal and sipping on the little whiskey that was left in his glass. Benjamin mentioning this Joseph Kabila and his rebel group had steered his thoughts back to Martina. He knew the mountains at which the gorillas resided were far from Goma, but he also knew they would have to pass through Goma to get there. *'Huh, they probably won't even come across any rebels,* he thought. He knew he had to shake himself out of it, he hardly knew Martina, and if she was prepared to take the risk, well, it was none of his business. So he had to force himself to consider, with a sigh.

He'd wanted to see the gorillas for years, and had always been keen on wildlife. But the opportunity had never arisen what with the war and all, but now wondered if his chance might come soon, now that the war is over, even though he knew it probably wasn't safe enough yet.

On that thought he grabbed his bottle, stood up, and left the small café to go to his room, unaware that his every move was being watched by the same young woman he'd just been thinking about.

After entering his room, he removed his shirt and hung it up in the small wardrobe that looked like an antique with the varnish peeling off in places. It for sure wasn't a five star hotel, but after the meal he'd just had, he wondered if it didn't deserve to be. It was old and in need of some repair, but as he sat on his bed, he knew at least it lived up to its name - Welcome Hotel.

His time in the café had passed quickly and it was now approaching 10.00 pm. He was considering an early night knowing he had a long journey tomorrow that would take him into the start of the Congo Basin and onto a dubious route.

Just was about to remove his trousers and climb onto the well tested bed that he had already given ten out of ten, but there was a very soft knock on the door. A confused but curious feeling overwhelmed him as he approached it. *Who could it be at this time of night, it must be someone at the wrong door,* he considered.

--Chapter Three--

SHE WAS THE last person he'd expected to see, but a rather obvious smile appeared on his face as he stood staring at Martina Gomez after he'd opened the door. She was dressed plainly in black jeans and a white T-shirt that did nothing to hide the size of her rather large breasts for a woman so slim. John had to resist just pulling her into the room and throwing her onto the bed, and it didn't help that during his time in the café and with a glass he'd just had, he'd almost managed to drink a half a bottle of whiskey.

'Hello, John. I was just wondering if you might need some help drinking that bottle of

Johnnie Walker,' Martina said, while not even trying to pull her line of sight away from John's muscular chest, and broad shoulders.

John was confused, but said what he wanted to say most of all. 'Well, you'd better come in then, Martina.' He scratched his head as he watched Martina place her small posterior on his bed. 'How'd you know, I mean, how'd you know I was staying here in this room, and how'd you know I had a bottle of Johnnie Walker?'

'Oh, John, so many questions and you haven't even given me a glass yet,' she said, now leaning back on his bed and being supported by her arms.

'Oh, I'm sorry, I guess you've caught me little off guard. So, are you going to tell me or am I going to have to guess,' he asked, now pouring a couple of drinks. 'Sprite okay, it's all I have,' he asked after taking out the partially empty can from the fridge.

'Yes, that'll be fine. I saw you in the café, John, and being treated like a king I might add.'

'Ah, yes, so you're also staying at this hotel?' he said, while passing her her drink and sitting down beside her, her perfume drawing him in, beating down on what little resistance he had.

'So, are you not going to explain?'

'Oh, you mean . . . there's nothing to explain. I'm a regular customer, that's all.' He didn't want to go into too much detail, because he didn't want to waste their time together talking about him. Plus he was sure she didn't want to hear about him beating up Bamboula and his men.

Martina wasn't convinced, but could see he didn't want to get into it so she left it at that.

'As it happens, I've been thinking about you quite a lot.'

'Oh, you have?' Martina said, now thinking this was far more interesting anyhow.

'Yes, I was worried, about you going into the jungle, I mean.'

That wasn't exactly what she was waiting to hear, but it was a start, she thought. 'Please John, I appreciate your concern, but I assure you there's no need. Let's just enjoy what little time we have together,' she said, now with her hand on his knee. 'We may never meet again after all,' she said, raising her glass.

John wasn't the type of person to miss an opportunity when it was staring him in the face, or offered to him on a plate. He lifted his glass and touched hers. 'Well, if you insist, Martina.' He was sure no man had refused her luring words and the way her eyes seem to drag you in, and he wasn't about to be the first. It was obvious enough to him by now why she'd come to his room, and it wasn't to discuss her going into the jungle. He felt the gentleman in him dispersing like water running down a stream and flowing into the river. He took her glass and placed it on the small fridge along with his. He then took her hand and guided to her feet. As tipsy as he was after drinking so much whiskey, he knew trying to peel off her tight fitting jeans, on the bed, would have without doubt been quite a challenge.

Martina rested her hands on John's strong shoulders while he undid the button on her jeans with such care. She then felt herself losing all control as he slowly pulled on her zip, and opened her jeans. As he pulled on her jeans with a graceful tug she knew she could be helping with her T-Shirt, but there was no hurry, and she was enjoying being undressed by the man she had found to be so handsome. She eventually raised her arms as John pulled her T-Shirt over her head and threw it across the room.

Bloody hell, John thought to himself as he stared at Martina's perfect body. Then, barely able to console himself, took off her bra and peeled off her panties. Martina wasn't a shy girl and was happy to stand there while he looked her up and down. John then whipped off his trousers and pants before pulling Martina towards him. He kissed her neck while slowly going down to her breasts, where he caressed her hard nipples using only his tongue. Martina's breathing had become loud and inconsistent as he ran his hands all over her body as if he was searching for a beauty spot or a small mole. Then just as their lips met, Martina felt John lift her as if she was a paper doll, with such ease, and with such grace. As he laid her on the bed Martina couldn't remember ever being handled with such care and consideration. The South American men she'd been with, and there'd been a few, had never treated her with such care. John continued to caress her body with his tongue and lips, and she lay there, now glad she'd come to his room. It wasn't long before she could feel his breath on her face and his manhood entering her while a feeling of ecstasy overwhelmed her. With every slow, gentle trust Martina released a groan, and as John quickened she cried out loud, not forgetting how thin the walls were, but just not caring. John lifted himself with his strong arms, looking down at Martina and wondering if it was possible for anyone to look so perfectly beautiful. He knew he had to try and hold back, but he also knew it weren't going to be easy. Just looking at her face and her beautiful brown eyes was more than enough, but feeling her smooth skin up against his and looking at her large beautiful breasts was too much. Then suddenly John stopped breathing before he let out the groan that he'd been trying to hold back.

It was over far too soon, but both laid there with a satisfied look on their face. Not a word was shared as they both lay there and fell asleep, John with his arm around Martina and both completely naked.

*

Meanwhile, in a slum not far away, where rats scampered the grounds looking for waste food, and where the homes were just wood and corrugated iron, somehow put together to make a shelter. Bamboula sat watching his twenty-inch black and white TV while drinking his home brew that smelled worse than the so called sewage system that fed the excrement into the Congo River. His wife, a fat woman weighing almost eighteen stone, lye on the floor with their child, and with only a sheet between her and the soft earth beneath it.

He sat relaxed on a small armchair where only the cushion that he sat on weren't actually torn. His skin was blacker than the blackest coal after spending most of his time in just a pair of shorts and no shirt. He was lean and muscular, without an ounce of fat and it wasn't because he didn't eat enough, because if he couldn't afford it, he'd steal it, from neighbours, friends or anyone he saw as easy or vulnerable. As low-lives went, Bamboula was at the top of the list.

The sound of tyres could be heard skidding on the soft ground just outside his shack. He felt sure he knew who it was so he got up from his armchair to go investigate. As he expected it was one of his men, or at least it was one of his friends who he liked to call one of his men.

A quite short guy that looked more than a little dim, climbed out of the beaten up old pickup. His black hair was thick but short, and looked like it had been placed on his head, rather than grown naturally. He also wore just a pair of shorts, though the back pockets were torn off, and his sandals were hanging onto his feet as if for dear life. Perspiration covered his body. 'He's back, Bamboula.'

Just by expression on his face Bamboula was sure he knew who he was talking about, and just then he caught his own reflection in the window of the pickup. He raged inside as he watched himself running his finger down the three inch scar that ran down his left cheek.

'Where?'

'I saw him at Nelson's bar first, so I followed him. He's staying at the Welcome Hotel again.'

The Journalists - Congo Rescue

Bamboula looked at his watch, which was actually just a child's watch, with Mickey Mouse hands. He'd stolen it from a kid only the day before. 'What time was this?'

'This afternoon.'

'So, why have you left it all this time to tell me, man?'

'Eh, I don't know, Bamboula.'

Bamboula knew he was a dimwit, but at least he'd gotten there eventually and told him that the Journalist was back. 'Okay, inform the men and bring them here. I'll be waiting.'

'Yes, Bamboula,' the dimwit said, feeling pleased with himself, and before climbing back into his truck and pulling away.

Bamboula knew it was almost midnight and he would probably have to wait until morning, but he didn't care. He'd waited a long time to get his revenge on the Journalist whom he was sure had had training, military training he suspected. But he was sure this time he'd be ready, unlike the first time when he thought he was dealing with just a journalist. He grabbed his machete, it was long and it was shiny. He'd been sharpening it for some time, and now it was like a razor and could cut through anything. While he'd sharpened it, night after night there had been only one thing on his mind - getting his revenge on the Journalist.

*

It was 6.00 am and the telephone that stood on the bedside cabinet, rang out loud. It was John's early morning call that he'd arranged with the receptionist the previous evening. He rolled over to answer it with his head throbbing; he knew the reason for that, and the nearly finished bottle of whiskey standing on the small fridge confirmed it 'You're early morning call, sir.' The young voice said at the other end of the line.'

'Thank you,' John said, in a voice that must have had the person wondering if he was okay.

It wasn't until he rolled back still half asleep that he realised he was alone. He wondered if it had been all a dream like the previous afternoon when he'd dreamed he was in the jungle. But if it had been, it had been one hell of a dream and one he wouldn't mind repeating. But he soon realised it couldn't have been a dream when he lay on the other pillow and smelled the same expensive perfume that he'd smelt at the bar after she'd approached him.

He remained quiet for a moment, listening for the sound of water running in the shower room, or even humming if she was putting on her makeup -

there wasn't a sound. He rolled out of the bed landing on his feet before going to the shower room to be sure. There could be no doubt, she wasn't there. He quickly slipped on his pants that had again convinced him it hadn't been a dream, because it was, they wouldn't have been lying on the floor in the middle of the room. Flickers of memory entered his mind as he started to make a cup of coffee. He used the kettle supplied by the hotel, and the sachets of coffee, sugar, and cream. Visions of her beautiful face and enchanting eyes rolled past his eyes, like an old film flickering and distorted as he was gradually waking up. Her perfume still strong, lingering as though she hadn't even left, but she had, and without saying a thing.

Knowing now that it wasn't a dream didn't help, because it still felt like a dream, just a dream, which had now ended. He still had to ask himself if it really happened, even though it was now clear in his head, him peeling off her panties and admiring her perfect body. Why would she have left without saying anything he wondered with an empty feeling churning in the depths of his stomach? He knew today he had to leave himself, which just added to the certainty; he knew he'd probably never see her again.

The Journalists - Congo Rescue

He shook his head knowing he had far more important things to focus on. Today he was going to be travelling to a city that had often been referred to as being the most dangerous city in the world, and he knew the route there was a favourite haunt for the rebels to hijack innocent people travelling back and forth to Kinshasa. The last thing he needed to be doing, was thinking about a woman he'd just met, and who had come to his room with one purpose in mind - having sex. It was good sex, and normally that would have been just fine, but as much as he hated to admit it, he really liked this woman.

Suddenly he felt an urge after he had made the coffee and was about to take a sip. After putting the cup down on the dressing unit he went back to the shower room. He stood there relieving himself when he noticed something on the shower room sink unit, something he was sure wasn't there before. Full of curiosity he picked it up to find out it was paper and had been folded in the shape of a heart. It was obvious enough who'd made it because other than the cleaning lady who had been older than his mother if she'd still been alive, no one else had entered his room, but it wasn't until he started to unfold it he realised it contained a small note.

The Journalists - Congo Rescue

Dear, John, thank you for such a wonderful evening. I just wanted to tell you that you're the nicest, most warmhearted caring man I have ever met, and I would have loved to of had the chance to get to know you better, but circumstances dictate I'm afraid. Don't concern yourself about me going into the jungle, as I can assure you I have it all under control. So this is goodbye and good luck my dear.

Martina.

Well, John thought, *at least now I know that I won't be seeing her again*. He knew it was for the better, and now it would be that little bit easier. So he took the small piece of paper and threw it in the small pink trash bin that was standing by his feet. He didn't want anything reminding him that he was now going to have to add Martina to a very long list of relationships that were just not going anywhere.

After he'd finished his coffee and taken a shower, he headed to the ground floor and to the small cafe to have breakfast.

He'd chosen to sit in the same place that he'd sat the previous evening - by the window. He sat there in complete silence, just looking around at the African ornaments and pictures for what seemed like ages, but was only a minute, before a young waiter, who John had guessed was probably the mornings cook too, came out of the kitchen.

'Good morning, Mr. John. How can I serve you?'

Serve me, John thought. *I'm not the king of Africa.* He wasn't so surprised that he knew his name; he was sure all the staff must know his name, complements of Benjamin without a doubt. The quite tall, very young waiter stood there looking as provisional as he could. He even had a small table cloth hanging from his arm. *Benjamin.* John knew it would have been the way he was taught, but felt it a little over the top for such a small cafe.

'I'll have the all day English breakfast, please.' John had decided a large breakfast would be wise knowing there was nowhere to eat between here and Goma, at least nowhere where he would want to eat.

'Yes, sir. Is that with coffee or tea?'

'Tea, please.

'Of course. sir.'

John almost laughed at the way the young waiter spoke in like a posh English accent, and as though this was the Savoy restaurant in London and not a small cafe in a two star hotel in the Democratic Republic of Congo.

The Journalists - Congo Rescue

John peered out the window just catching the sun rising from the back of a shabby, looking store that stood just the other side of the street. The street, which was just red dirt, was quiet, with just the odd truck passing by on it, the vehicle's wheels jumping up and down as they passed over the uneven surface. He'd noticed a few specs of rain on the window which had given him some concern. He knew his route to Goma was partially dirt track, in fact, at least fifty miles was just gravel mixed with the soft, jungle soil, which when wet, was more than a little difficult to pass. He'd hired himself a Landrover Defender with four wheel drive, but knew even that might struggle if it rained.

His breakfast had soon arrived and looked quite nice. The way it was placed on the plate as it smiled at him was kind of appetizing, but whether it was going to be enough to carry him through the long journey that he knew he had ahead of him was doubtful. Two fried eggs and a couple of strips of bacon, which made the smiling mouth and was barely enough to feed a cat. He knew the two rounds of toast that sat on a small side plate would help a little, but if it wasn't for the waiter's smile that was full of pride, he might have ordered the same again. 'Thank you,' he said, not sure if the smile he'd given the waiter, come cook, was convincing enough.

--*Chapter Four*--

JOHN HAD FINISHED his breakfast in about one second flat, before gulping down his tea. He was now determined to get this last part of his assignment finished as soon as possible. He'd gone back to his room to collect his rucksack before checking out of the hotel. While he'd checked out he had considered asking if the South American's had checked out yet. But he'd decided the less he knew, the better.

He'd disposed of the peace of rag that he'd used to check the oil and water even though he'd been sure that it must be okay, with it being a hire vehicle.

His face cringed slightly as he put some effort into checking the wheel nuts, though being two feet long the wheel brace had given him plenty of leverage making it that much easier. He was also glad it was long because at the side of his eye, he'd noticed four men coming towards him and just by their smell he was sure they were not there to assist him. As he stood up straight he saw they were obviously not there to have a chat about the weather either.

He gripped the wheel brace tightly as he stood looking at Bamboula and his pals. He'd noticed the long and rather shiny machete held by Bamboula, and had noticed the other three were also armed with knives.

'Hey, guys, listen, I don't have time for this now, can't you come back another time.' John said, then continued to tighten the wheel nuts.

Bamboula was obviously pissed and not at all impressed at John's loose words and don't-give-a-shit attitude. He was full of rage, his blood pumping fast.

'I guess not then,' John said, now holding the wheel brace and approaching Bamboula and his men. He'd already come to the conclusion that

The Journalists - Congo Rescue

Bamboula, especially now he was holding a machete, would probably be a bit of a hand full, but as for his pals, well, he had to wonder why they were even there at all. They all had their mean face's on, or at least three of them did, but as for the dimwit, John couldn't read him at all.

'Listen, guys, is there not enough pain and suffering in this country without people like you adding to it, why can't you just live your lives peacefully like normal human beings, instead of all this violence.'

The dimwit started to lower his knife, until he glanced at Bamboula, then just as quickly he lifted it again.

John knew the best thing to do was to get Bamboula riled, though judging by his face that wasn't going to take much. He knew that way he would charge in, but without any real control. 'So, Bamboula what do your wife think of your new scar, I bet she likes it, hey.'

Bamboula said nothing, he didn't need to. John could read him like a book. Just as John was hoping he charged in holding his machete high. His pals figured he could take the westerner who was just holding a wheel brace, so they held back. Bamboula brought the machete down hard, while with both hands John raised the wheel brace to guard himself. Steel met with steel, but the wheel brace was hardened steel, the machete wasn't. It snapped like a twig, the broken end flying through the air and landing some distance away. John then swung the wheel brace back handed, catching Bamboula on the side of the head. He went down hard, and remained down, lying in the dirt, blood dripping from his ear.

His pals were about to charge in too, at least two of them were, the dimwit just stood there looking gormlessly at his pals.

'Really!' John said, stopping them in their tracks. They were obviously not keen, they looked down at their so called leader who lay motionless, and silent. They then threw away their knives and left the scene, leaving Bamboula lying there with his mouth wide open, and breathing heavily.

John was glad it was over, because now he could get on with the job he was being paid for. He opened the back door to the vehicle and threw the wheel brace onto the back seat, thinking he might need it again, and nut to check the wheel nuts. Then climbing behind the steering wheel he turned the key in the ignition, backed out of the hotel car park and headed towards the n1 highway that would take him north, and on to Goma.

The Journalists - Congo Rescue

Because of Bamboula and his friends, John was running a little later than he'd hoped. He was now on the n1 highway, but the traffic wasn't as it would have been if he hadn't been delayed. It was now quite busy and he knew the reason for that was because the domestic airport that was only twenty miles ahead. However, John was happy enough knowing he was travelling at a steady sixty miles an hour on the six lane highway.

John looked up to the sky that was far more concerning than the traffic had been, which now was just a trickle after passing the airport. He had considered taking an internal flight to Goma, but he'd seen the planes, and heard of the wreckages that apparently were scattered all over the Congo Basin. International standards didn't apply here and he was sure they probably never would.

An hour and a half into the Journey and the clouds above were dark. John felt sure it was only a matter of time before they would burst their contents all over the route to Goma. He also knew the two lane road that he was driving on would soon become nothing but a dirt track and if it was to rain, it would be nothing but a pool of slushy mud that even the best vehicles would struggle to pass.

Winding down the window and lighting up a cigarette he had to make a decision. He knew there were two or three motels on the route where he could stop and wait to see what happened. The problem with that idea was, if it did rain, it could rain for days and he'd be stranded in what he knew were pretty awful motels. Or he could risk it knowing that might mean getting stuck on the road, for what could also be for days. The only thing that was giving him some reprieve was that the rain might just keep the rebels away. He was travelling light and had no valuables on him; even his watch was an old one that he'd decided to wear knowing he might come across some rebels on the way. It wouldn't have been the first time he'd run into rebels, and knew as long as you stayed calm and did everything they asked they would normally wave you on.

He also knew that wasn't always the case, especially if you were a woman, an attractive woman. He was well aware that women were constantly dragged out of their vehicles and into the now quite thick vegetation, and if they were with their husbands, he would be made to stay with the vehicle and listen to her screams.

The engine roared as he put his foot down hard on the accelerator after seeing the dirt track ahead, knowing it only went for about fifty miles he threw what was left of his cigarette out the window and wound it up tight. His plan was to travel as far as he could in as little time as he could before the heavens opened. As he hit the dirt track the vehicle shook as it arrived at the uneven surface. He noticed a few cars coming the other way, but he was sure he was probably the only vehicle heading north. He looked in his rear view mirror and saw nothing. *Was it because they had more sense,* he asked himself. It was too late now; turning around on this road was far too risky. If he was to get stuck he'd almost definitely be hit by one of the oncoming vehicles that were now passing him at high speed, obviously trying to get off the dirt track before the heavens erupted.

Suddenly the awful motels seemed quite attractive as the view ahead became murky. He had to slam on his breaks as he approached the wall of rain that had blanked out any view of the track ahead, and as he hit the wall the noise was deafening as the rain hit his vehicle with a constant clang. He was almost brought to a standstill because of the view, or lack of it. Looking at the speedometer he could see the needle juddering just above the ten-miles an hour, and knew he had at least another thirty-five more miles to travel before the road would improve, it was not great.

He plodded along as well as he could knowing he had to at least try to keep the vehicle on the track. It wasn't easy with the vehicle slipping and sliding on the now soft surface which was just getting worse. Even with the four-wheel drive vehicle it was virtually useless. 'God damn it,' he said to himself, while hitting his hand hard on the steering wheel. *Shit, I should have known better.*

He carried on knowing he had absolutely no choice in the matter. One mile at a time, one bend at a time where he had to manoeuvre the vehicle even more carefully. He'd been driving at ten miles an hour for at least an hour, when he just happened to peer out through the passenger side window where the view was slightly better because of the trees shading the rain. He'd carried on for a few metres, not wanting to stop, knowing it was the worst thing you could do in these conditions, but knowing he had to, he had no choice. He'd seen a vehicle that had run off the track, it was just a four door saloon, and sitting in the back he was sure he'd spotted a child. 'Oh shit,' he said, out loud while again hitting his steering wheel with some force.

He brought the vehicle to a stop, even knowing pulling away from a standstill in these conditions was never easy. Reluctantly, he opened the door and got out, he was drenched within seconds and as he looked down at his boots he could see they were under at least six-inches of mud. He waded through the mud one long stride at a time until he saw the saloon just at the side of the track. '*What the bloody hell am I doing,* he asked himself, knowing that a local would have probably just carried on. He stepped off the track and onto the undergrowth where at least the ground was a little more firm, though still very soft.

The question he'd asked himself only seconds ago was soon answered. He now knew what the bloody hell he was doing there when he saw the young child that he guessed was only about three, crying in the back seat. He was now glad that he'd stopped. Reading about a young child dying in the back seat of a saloon, would have for sure played on his mind for some time.

He tried the back door, but it was locked. He then started to make his way to the other side of the car passing the boot to the sound of squelching beneath his feet. But he soon stopped after noticing the car was in a very precarious position, it was on a ledge which John guessed descended quite a few metres, though not willing to lean over to see. He knew he had to get the kid out quickly before the car slid over the edge with the help from the soft drenched soil and wet leaves and grass, and the fact it was still raining heavily made it all the more urgent. He trudged around to the driver's side, and to the driver's door, where he now saw what looked like a young woman, out cold, with her head leaning on the steering wheel. The door was locked. He had to think quickly, he knew he had to smash a window and the wheel brace was the first thing to enter his mind, but whether there was time to fetch it or not was debatable, but he knew he had to try. He could hear the child's crying, getting louder as he was wading through the mud again. He didn't know whether it was a girl or boy at this stage, but he guessed she or he must have thought he was leaving them.

He made it back and opened the back door while trying not to slip over. He grabbed the wheel brace and made his way back to the car, while hoping at the same time someone would pass by that could help him, not that he thought they would anyhow.

The child's crying eased as he approached the car again. John had considered securing the car first, he was sure just the force of him breaking the window could cause the vehicle to slide over the edge. He knew this wasn't an option, he had no rope, and using the vegetation would take too long. He then had to make a very difficult decision, who to help first. It wasn't easy, but he'd decided to help the young woman who he'd assumed must be the mother.

He could see she was leaning on the steering wheel which was good because her face would be clear of the glass when it smashes. John didn't hang around, he knew he couldn't. He swung back with the wheel brace almost as far as he did when he wacked Bamboula with it. The window smashed easily enough, so he unlocked the door and opened it. Without hesitation, he lifted the young woman out of the car, and he was about to lay her on the wet ground when he saw what he now knew was a young boy, climbing out of the car all by himself. He now looked calm, and as though he was on an adventure, with a slight smile as he looked up at John. John headed towards the road feeling sure the young boy would follow; he did, still smiling as he waded through the mud in his underpants. John was impressed and felt he'd been brought up well. John opened the back door where he laid the young woman on the back seat, who he'd guessed was in her mid twenties. He checked her breathing first by putting his ear near her mouth, and then checked her pulse. Little thing's he'd learned in the forces, but had come in handy several times since he'd been a journalist. He felt sure she was alright, so he closed the back door behind him.

He looked down at the young boy who couldn't have been more than three, and who was covered in mud, just like himself, and with the usual smile on his face. John was sure it was because he knew that his mother was in safe hands now.

'Come on chappie, let's get you into the car,' John said, with a warm smile and a wink. He knew cleaning him up a little before putting him into the car would be impossible, so he lifted him and passed him through the driver's side door, before sitting on the passenger side seat. He then climbed in himself. John started the vehicle while at the same time praying that he could pull away. He glanced at the young boy, who was staring at him with what now seemed like a permanent smile. He ruffled the young boys short curly hair a little before putting the car in gear and releasing the clutch, and to his relief, it pulled away just fine.

After around thirty minutes of driving no quicker than ten miles an hour, to John's relief the rain eased, and just as quickly the sun shone through the clouds as they parted revealing a beautiful blue sky. But as happy as that had made him feel, it also gave him cause for concern. He knew this might bring out the rebels. The last thing he needed now, especially with a young woman lying on the back seat. He was sure it wouldn't have mattered to them that she hadn't even regained consciousness; in fact, he felt sure they'd probably like the fact that she hadn't regained consciousness.

At as fast a speed as he could he continued, but the track was still wet and on the occasion the vehicle was still trying to run off into the vegetation. But he was now sure it couldn't be far before they reached the main road.

Suddenly, John began to feel a little feverish and his nose started running.

'It's the rain.' A voice said from behind him.

'Ah, your back, I knew you would be, just didn't know when.' John replied, looking in the rearview mirror. 'What was the rain?'

'The reason you're sick.'

'Ah, I see.'

'What happened?'

'You run off the road - you were lucky I saw you.'

'Thank you,' The young women said, while looking at her young boy, who was now sound asleep and lying on John's lap. 'That's so strange.'

'You're welcome, what's so strange?'

'My boy, he doesn't make friends easily, he seems to be scared of all grownups.'

'Scared, no, he's had a permanent smile on his face ever since I pulled you out of the car.'

'Well, that is strange.'

'Not really, he obviously loves you very much.'

'You think that's why, because you saved me.'

'Could be, if what you say is true about him not liking adults, losing you would have been all the more daunting for him. Has he seen death before? I mean has he seen a dead person...

'Yes, plenty, this is the Congo.'

'Well, that explains it, he thought he'd lost you then I came along to help. John said, while wiping his nose with his hand.

'Where you going?'

'Goma.'

'Goma's another one hundred miles, you need to get out of those wet clothes or you will become very ill. You should stay at my place, it's only another ten miles.'

'Ah, I appreciate that, but I have a schedule to keep, I need to get to Goma.'

Even if it kills you, hah, up to you 'What do you do?'

'I'm a journalist; I'm here to report on the Aids pandemic.'

The Journalists - Congo Rescue

If you don't get out of those clothes, you'll be reporting on nothing. 'Turn left here, it's just a mile down this track. 'I suppose I should at least ask my rescuer his name.'

John laughed slightly before saying. 'It's John.' He knew he probably should ask her name, but figured he'd probably never see her again and, well, she's not the first person he'd rescued.

'Well, thank you again, John,' she said sincerely. She wanted to tell him her name but concluded if he wanted to know he would have asked.

John just nodded.

'Just here John, you can pull in here.'

John did as he was asked, only to be faced with a shabby, but quite large wooden country house. Outside sitting on a large porch at the front of the house was at least a dozen people, 'You have a large family.'

'Not really, it's just unlike *you*, all the family lives together in the same house. I hope you allow me to introduce you to all of them; it's just that if you don't I won't hear the last of it.'

John was a little reluctant, but knew it was the right thing to do; he had just rescued her after all, and possibly saved her life if the car had gone over the edge. He opened his door feeling more than a little groggy. Then stepped out after the young woman had removed her boy, but suddenly he came over dizzy and fell to his knees.

'I told you so.'

--*Chapter Five*--

'**I TOLD YOU** so' were the last words that John could remember after waking up in a cold sweat, and lying in unfamiliar surroundings. He looked around the large room that he'd found himself in with some interest. Large beams stretched across the ceiling supporting the dark wood floor boards to the room above. Wood panelling and a couple of African style pictures decorated the walls, but other than a small table that sat at the far end of the room, it was bare. Then he just happened to glance to his right at about the same level as where his head lie on the pillow, to see the young boy sitting there with a smile so wide. John couldn't help but smile back at the sight that had been with him since he'd rescued him and his mother.

'Mama!' the young boy called out.

It wasn't long before the door opened and the young woman entered. She'd obviously had a shower and a change of clothes.

Her hair was straight and rested on her shoulders, she wore white beads around her neck and the same colour beads were clipped to her ears. Her blouse was black with gold buttons, and she wore black jeans with a thick leather belt. John was a little taken aback, he hadn't quite realised just how lovely she was.

'How you feeling, John. I did try to warn you.'

'Yes, you did, and it's just as well I passed out here and not on the way to Goma.' He said, feeling very grateful. 'I'm sorry I should have listened, and I'm so sorry I haven't even asked your name.'

'It's Maria, and this is Gia, and yes, you should have listened,' she said, looking at her young boy. 'He loves you, John. He hasn't left your side since we placed you on this bed.' Maria shook her head. 'Really, I don't understand, he's never like this.'

'It must be my warm, friendly face.' John said, grinning.

Maria laughed.

'What about his father, is he not close to him?' John felt he had to ask, even though he knew it was none of his business.

'He was never there for his son.' Maria paused.

John waited.

'He's not a nice man.' Maria continued, a single tear running down her cheek. 'He's a cruel, mean man, who has never done a hard day's work in his life.'

It didn't take a genius to figure out that they were no longer a couple. 'Does he not visit sometimes?'

'Oh, yes, he visits, but not to see me and not even to see his son. He hangs out with a group of men who are no better than him - they're nothing but a bunch of thieves. They steal from the vulnerable and weak. If they resist, he or one of his men shoots them.' Maria took a deep breath, her bottom lip quivering. 'He shot my grandfather. He was the only one brave enough to face him. He just asked him to leave. He wasn't being aggressive, he just asked him to leave, and not to come back. Amos, shot him, I can still see the grin on his face as he did it. I hate him so much.' Maria said, while trembling with rage, but also sadness as she thought of her grandfather.

John wanted to climb out of his bed and hold her. It was a story he'd heard so many times during his travels, bullies, he hated bullies. He sounded just like Bamboula and so many others. A man who has nothing so to make his life seem meaningful he picks on vulnerable people who can't defend themselves.

'You said he visits, but not to see you, or Gia.' John said, looking at the young boy who was now looking at his mother.

Maria wipes her nose. 'I'm sorry John; I don't mean to bother you with my problems.'

'It's fine,' John said, he could see she needed to talk about it, to get it off her chest.

'He comes to steal our food stocks. We are poor people, John; we barely have enough to feed ourselves.'

John was taking an instant dislike to this Amos, even though he hadn't even met him; he had met plenty like him. But not Maria, he wasn't taking an instant dislike to her. He felt himself warming to her, not just because she was a very attractive young woman, but he prided himself on knowing when a woman was descent or not. He was sure she was, and a descent mother too, just looking at how well behaved her son was - was more enough to convince him of that. 'Have you not tried telling the police?'

'This isn't England, John. I'm sorry, I guess you are British, you definitely sound British.'

John smiled. 'Yes, I'm British - you've met British people before?'

'Some, British, American, European.' Maria could see the look of surprise on John's face. 'I sometimes work as a tour guide to bring in a little extra money.'

'Really, but isn't that dangerous.' John knew it must be but had to ask.

'Um, not really, I only take them to see the sights of Goma, and the surrounding area. I don't take them into the jungle or anywhere dangerous like that.'

'Sights of Goma, what the hell does Goma have to offer to make people travel half way around the world to see - mass graves or something like that.'

'Exactly, it's the reputation it has that attracts people. They like to be able to say they've visited the most dangerous city in the world, and survived, and of course they also come to see the volcano.'

'I'm sorry, but I can never understand people like that, they live in countries where they can venture out at night without getting murdered or raped and just to get some kind of thrill they come to places like this. What a mad world it is.'

'Um, but I'm not complaining.' Maria insists, shrugging her shoulders.

'No, and I don't blame you Maria. So, it's a waste of time going to the police, right, about Amos I mean.'

'Absolutely, they're just as bad if not worse,' Maria shrugs again. 'That is, of course, unless you have plenty of money.'

John had to ask, but he was sure this was the case. Just like most countries in Africa, money, and power is everything. If you don't have these you're as good as nothing, and no one will help you. He'd known this for many years now, but it still really gets his back up sometimes. He started to sit up; he'd had enough of lying in bed.

'Where are *you* going, John?' Maria asked, placing her hands on his shoulders.

'Sorry Maria, but I can't stay here. I have to get to Goma.'

'But you can't . . .

The Journalists - Congo Rescue

John soon comes over dizzy again. 'What the hell.'

'It's what you picked up in the rain, could be anything, I've given you some medicine, but it will take time. Besides, it's now getting dark, you don't won't to be travelling to Goma at night, it's far too dangerous.'

John knew she was right about travelling to Goma at night, but he hadn't realised it was so late. 'What is, the time?'

'6.00 o'clock in the evening.'

'Wow, I didn't realise, I must have slept like a baby.' Something John knew he seldom did. Usually he'd be woken up after dreaming about something from his past, usually during his time in the forces. He'd seen things that would haunt anyone's dreams, and for most, give them nightmares.

'You must be hungry, John. Would you like something to eat?'

'Yes, I am a little hungry - thanks that would be great.'

Maria was happy to take care of John. He did rescue her after all, but it wasn't just that. She could see he was a good man, and had to ignore her feelings as she looked at his handsome face. The fact that he was obviously quite a bit older than her, she'd guessed probably about ten years, didn't matter a hoot.

After watching Maria leave the room, and glancing over to where her young boy sat quiet as a mouse while playing with a small toy on his lap, a thought had entered his head. He searched his eyes around the room looking for his GPS phone. He knew he had to contact his agency to let them know he would be delayed. He eventually spotted it on the small table at the far end of the room.

Turning again to look at the young boy, he then pointed at his phone. Without hesitation the young boy placed his small toy on the chair he was sitting on, and made his way to the small table.

He passed John his phone, and John thanked him. The smile on the young boy's face was wider than ever, as if he'd just done a huge thing for John, and not just passed him his phone. John was becoming quite attached to the young boy, but knew anyone would, other than his father of course. What kind of man was he, John considered, not to care about his own boy, and a boy who was so cute.

Holding his GPS tracking phone firmly he scrolled through his contacts looking for Jonathan. It didn't take long, because he had very few contacts, and also very few friends. He'd put it down to his career choices, now a journalist and before that in the forces - always travelling from one dangerous country to the next.

He couldn't help but spot his best friend's name just under Jonathan's. His best friend and only real friend. A man he knew he could rely on, at any time, night or day, and in any situation. He decided he probably should give him a call soon too.

Knowing the time difference was only one hour, he tapped on Jonathan's name, knowing it was around 5.00 o'clock in the UK. The phone at the other end rang only twice before a quite posh accent said. 'John, I wasn't expecting to hear from you so soon, I do hope you're coping okay?'

John knew he'd be surprised; he doesn't usually contact him until the assignment has been completed and, sometimes not until he'd arrived back in the UK. 'Hi, Jonathan, yes, I'm coping fine.' John was sure he was talking about his assignment, which reminded him of the sights he'd seen at the hospital. 'I'm just calling to say there will be some delay.'

'Oh, there will, well, I hope you haven't got yourself involved in some kind of war again. You just need to complete the assignment and get yourself back here.' Jonathan had lost count of how many times John had made enemies of warlords, cruel generals, and corrupt officials. He respected him for it, but was sure that someday he would bite on a little more than he could chew. He didn't want to lose his best man.

'No, Jonathan, I've just come down with something, a bad flu or something, you know how easy it is to pick up a germ here, especially when it rains.' John didn't want to go into too much detail, but felt he may have already said too much.

'Rain, I'm sure you had more sense than to be out in that dreadful rain, John. Oh, gosh, you know it carries more deceases than I can count on both of my hands, don't you.'

'Well eh…'

'Don't tell me - rescuing a damsel in distress again.'

'Well, as it happens.'

'Oh, John, this is how it always starts, haven't you learned yet. Soon you'll be fighting off vicious rebels, or Islamic terrorist that mean to do her harm. It's always the same. I respect what kind of man you are, John, but you can't save the world, as much as I'm sure you'd like to.'

'Don't you think you're being a little dramatic, Jonathan,' John said, though knowing what Jonathan was saying was actually true. It did always seem to start with a woman. He suddenly found himself shaken a thought from his head. He'd been thinking of someone he hadn't even met yet. He had been thinking about Amos.

'You, tell me, John, am I really being dramatic?'

'Well, eh, maybe not, but not this time, Jonathan.' John sincerely hoped, with a swift cross of his fingers. 'As soon as I'm well enough I'll be heading to Goma to complete the assignment.'

'Well, I sincerely hope so, John.'

'So, where have you sent my pal, Jonathan?'

'Ah, Christopher, you mean.'

'Yes, Chris, somewhere nice I hope.'

'Well, I wouldn't call it nice exactly, he got the Somalia job.'

'Ah, the western family that was murdered, bloody place, who would want to go there for a vacation,' John said, while remembering what Maria had said only moments before, about people being attracted to places with a reputation.

'As I've said so many times to you and to Chris, why is not our concern, we're just there to report on what happened and no more.'

John felt sure that that would not be enough for Chris; he knew they were alike, in just about every way. He also knew he wouldn't want to be the bastards that had done it, not if Chris was to find out who it was. 'I wouldn't worry Jonathan, I'm sure he'll want to get out of that place as soon as possible.'

'Um, I hope you're right, John. You two are my best men and also my biggest headache. Just keep me informed, okay.'

'Yes, will do, Jonathan,' he said before ending the call. John knew why they were his best men. He knew Jonathan could send them to places where other journalist's wouldn't go. John passed his phone back to the young boy while looking him over. He couldn't help but feel sorry for him, especially now, knowing his father's story.

At that moment the door opened and Maria entered carrying a large tray of food. She placed it on the same small table where John's phone now lay again. 'I hope it's to your liking; there's chicken and there's pork and some vegetables,' Maria said, while feeling sure he would like it.

'Well, it smells good so that's a good start.' John got out of bed slowly in case he comes over dizzy again. He sat down at the small table with a satisfying smile on his face. 'Um, that does look good,' he said, pleasing Maria no end.

Maria sat on the bed and watched John empty the plate, before helping him back into bed. 'Now you need to rest, I'm sure by morning's light you'll feel much better.' Maria then took her son's hand and led him out of the room while telling him that John needs to rest.

John was left to his thoughts, and he was thinking about his best friend Chris. He was sure Chris's assignment had all the signs of a small terrorist group, or part of a larger terrorist group, ether way he was sure it was terrorists. Al Shabab, he considered, although for them to target just a single western family was unlikely. Maybe a small local group who had been disillusioned with the local government there, he knew it wouldn't take much, not in Somalia. He knew by them targeting tourists, it would be the government that paid the price in lost revenue. But that didn't take away the fact that poor innocent westerners were killed just for being in the wrong place at the wrong time. That didn't sit well with him and he knew it wouldn't sit well with Chris.

--Chapter Six--

THE NEXT MORNING John opened his eyes to be looking down the barrel of an AK47. A quite tall, if not lanky Congolese man wearing shabby clothes, stared at him with a look of surprise after finding a westerner in the bed, and achievement, as though he'd just apprehended a US General. He wore a grin that was showing of his yellow teeth, a grin that John wanted to rip from his face.

John wasn't sure if it was Amos or one of his pals, it didn't matter; he was pointing the gun in his face. John grinned back at him, he wanted to confuse him rather than do the obvious - shake with fear. Then, John glanced to the right, and as John was hoping the man did the same, giving John just enough time to grab the gun by the barrel and pull it towards him and the man too, though making sure at the same time, the gun was no longer pointing directly at him. He grabbed the man by the hair before putting him in a headlock as he fell forward. Then, with a sudden movement of his entire body, John broke his neck. It was over in a flash, it had to be so the man never got the chance to make a noise. John was sure there were others.

'Bifuasa!' a man called with a hint of anger in his croaky voice.

John laid the man's head down on the floor before grabbing his gun and peering out of the window. He rubbed his eyes some, still feeling groggy and half asleep. He could see another guy waiting outside, but he was sure there was more than one. They'd obviously seen his car so they knew he was there, somewhere.

John was a little surprised to see the man standing in the open, though he wouldn't be expecting his man to be dead. It was just a matter of time before he started to get suspicious. John had very little time to decide his next move. He was too slow, the man had grabbed the old woman, John was sure it must be Maria's grandmother and the wife of the man who was killed by Amos. John wasn't sure if this was Amos either, but he obviously wasn't too smart. He'd grabbed the woman, but held her to the side of him and rested his arm on her shoulder. The poor woman was clearly petrified, and probably thinking of her husband.

John had a clear shot, and there was no time for hesitation, the guy might come to his senses and actually hide behind the old girl. John did have to consider what was going on out of sight, but one less man to deal with could only be a good thing. John shot him between the eyes and he dropped to the floor in a heap.

John could hear sounds of feet on the floor boards just outside the door, and also whispering a little further away. He knew there was more than one, maybe two. He was also sure the family was in some danger, now that they knew they weren't dealing with just anyone. The longer he stayed in the room the more time they would have to organise, this he had to avoid. Using the barrel of his gun while using the wall for cover, he opened the door wide. Shots were fired, piercing the wooden walls as splinters of wood darted across the room. But now John had a better idea as to where the men were. He could tell at least from the angle at which the bullets hit the wall they had been shot from directly in front of the door, but at some distance away. He peered through the window again; the only place it could have come from was behind their vehicle which was parked some ten meters away, but as he'd guessed, directly in front of the door.

John recognised the vehicle, it was a Toyota Landcruiser Jeep, he'd driven one before and knew it was a decent vehicle, but more importantly, he knew exactly where the fuel tank was, and it was on the side he needed it to be. He aimed the AK-47 low, just behind the rear wheel. He was sure it wouldn't take much to penetrate the panel, or the tank, the vehicle was as old as the hills that surrounded their location. He shot just a couple of rounds so as to conserve his ammo, and the rear of the vehicle soon became a ball of flames, leaping about four feet in the air. The guy who John knew was hiding behind the vehicle had also turned into a ball of flames, and was zigzagging away from the house while screaming relentlessly before he hit the dust.

Meanwhile, Maria and her family were witnessing a show they'd wanted to watch for some time. John was picking them off one by one and he hadn't even left the room that he'd spent the night in.

Unfortunately, Amos was still standing, even if he was, shaken in his boots. 'Who the hell is this guy!' Amos shouted, while looking at Maria.

She just shrugged. She was as surprised as anyone; she'd thought he was just a journalist.

Suddenly Amos did what any desperate man would do. He grabbed Maria, dragged her in front of the house and held his pistol to her head. 'Come out with your hands in the air, and leave the gun inside, or I'll splatter her head all over this land.'

John knew he would, he'd met men like him, dozens of them. He had no choice; he laid the gun on the bed and exited the room slowly with his hands in the air.

Amos was shocked to see he was a westerner, but now he was looking forward to killing him. He'd never killed a westerner before.

'Okay, I'm here, you can let her go.'

'No,' Maria shrieked. A feeling of guilt overwhelmed her knowing he was only here because he'd rescued her; she knew he didn't deserve to die.

Amos let her go, but she refused to move. 'No,' she yelled again looking directly into Amos's eyes, pleading with him while standing between him and John. She saw only coldness in his eyes; she knew her pleading was to no avail. Suddenly, Amos pushed her to the floor while she was still screaming. He then aimed his pistol at John and there was a shot, it was loud, deafening. Maria turned to John, he was still standing and his arms were still raised. She was confused, she looked at Amos and as she did, he fell to his knees, blood pouring from his mouth. Maria glanced over to where her grandmother stood. She still held her husband's gun up high.

John had seen her grab the gun, and he'd felt if anyone should kill Amos it should be her. There was a small thud as Amos's face hit the dirt.

Maria picked herself up off the ground and run towards her grandmother. The old girl was trembling, though with a smile as wide as her face as she saw her granddaughter running towards her. Maria took the gun from her and they embraced tightly. John felt a warm feeling in his heart as the family came together in front of the house. Even Gia came out from where he'd been hiding, but he headed straight for John and wrapped his little arms around his legs. John picked him up and gave him a kiss on the cheek, then Gia wrapped his arms around his neck. Maria was besieged with emotion as she watched her son. She soon joined them wrapping her arms around the both of them.

'How can I ever thank you enough?' Maria asked sincerely, looking into John's eyes and resting her hands on his shoulders.

John just smiled. Then, as he lowered Gia to the floor the rest of the family gathered around him. The men shook his hand and the women hugged him tightly. The old girl said something in her local dialogue, John couldn't understand. Maria translated it for him.

'She wants to prepare you a special breakfast; she hopes you can stay long enough, John.'

John smiled, and simply said. 'Oh, okay then.' John was feeling more than a little famished and welcomed a nice breakfast before he had to leave.

The old lady smiled while heading towards the kitchen area, Maria took John's hand and led him onto the porch. After sitting him down on their most comfortable chair, she asked. 'Would you like a coffee, John?' Even though she knew it was hardly enough after all he'd done.

John hesitated. 'That's okay, you needn't bother, just a glass of water will do.'

'It's no bother John, it's the least I can do for the man who has saved my life twice.'

The Journalists - Congo Rescue

'Well, I wouldn't say that Maria, I pulled you out of your car that's all, and it was your grandmother who saved you the second time.'

'Ah, but John you don't know - my uncle went to fetch the car this morning, but it was in a thousand pieces at the bottom of a steep gorge. So, there, you did save my life, and my grandmother would never have done what she did if not for you, so, twice it is, now about that coffee?'

'Well, I guess it's the very least that I deserve, then,' John said, even though all he'd been trying to do was avoid the coffee, he'd tasted the coffee here many times, and had had to throw it away each time.

Maria headed to the kitchen area which was outside to the left of the house to make John's coffee. John sat in the very comfortable arm chair on the porch, just watching the family get on with their lives despite there being three bodies lying dead on the dirt. It was obvious that they had seen dead bodies before, probably plenty. This was the Congo and this was how it was. Life was cheap and death was all around them. Even Gia played ball with himself, kicking the ball past his own father who lay dead on the ground.

It had reminded John of a mission he was on, when in the Para's. A mission that would haunt his dreams like so many missions he was on did. This mission was in Mali, southern Sahara desert. A British missionary was there to teach the ways of Christ. It was John's mission to get him out of there before he started a civil war. They had arrived too late; the fool had gotten the whole village killed. There were bodies everywhere, mothers, fathers, the elderly, young children and babies just lying in the sand under the desert sun, and a swarm of flies. In his dream one of the babies would open his eyes and ask John why it had taken him so long to get there.

It was at that point when John would wake up in a cold sweat. He often wondered why he did the things he did, and the answer was always the same - because he can. He was trained to the highest level and more. He was the best man in the Paratroopers and the best man in the Special Forces. It was though he was born for this, born to be the best. What would be the point if he didn't use his unique skills to help the weak and vulnerable?

He was being reminded right now, just why he did it, as he scanned his eyes around at the family that were making him feel so welcome. Just looking at their smiles, and hearing their laughter after he had helped to dispose of a group of men that were making their lives and so many other lives, miserable.

John watched as Maria approached him, a beautiful young woman who had stood between him and Amos knowing that might mean her being killed. It was something John would not forget.

'Here's your coffee, John.'

'Thank you,' he said, with a warm smile and just a little dread. He smelled the coffee and was pleasantly surprised. 'Ah, you've done this before haven't you?'

Maria smiled 'Yes, it was part of my training to be a tour guide, to make coffee for the tourists - they're mostly westerners,' she shrugged

John took a sip. 'Um, that is good, thank you so much.'

'You're more than welcome, John. I just wish I could do more, I feel I owe you so much.'

'You don't owe me anything, sweetheart. Would you sit here for a while?' John asked, pointing to a small wooden chair that was next to his armchair.

Maria gladly did as he asked.

John wanted to know more about her. 'So, have you always lived here?' A rather obvious question to start with but that didn't matter.

The Journalists - Congo Rescue

'No, it's been around a year since we left my home in the Shaba Province. It was so beautiful there, our farm was big, and the ground was so fertile, and mountains surrounded the entire area, not like this place, we were never rich John, but we were making a comfortable living.'

John scratches his head. 'So what happened, Maria?'

'Joseph Kabila happened.'

'Ah, the warlord you mean.' John could remember Benjamin talking about him at the welcome hotel; he'd told him what kind of man he was, and had mentioned the atrocities he'd committed.

'Yes, that Joseph Kabila, we had to flee for our lives as he took over our farm and most of that area. He's a cruel, ruthless man, much worse than Amos was, and he's very powerful.

John knew he must be powerful but was curious as to why. 'Powerful, in what way, Maria?'

'Well, powerful because he has thousands of rebels that follow him religiously and would follow him to the end of the world. The government has promised that they will win our land back, but there's no hunger for more war, and they know if they try to attack him many thousands of good men will die.'

The Journalists - Congo Rescue

John knew for his rebels to follow him so religiously there had to be a reason and it wouldn't have been because of his good looks. In John's experience there was usually only one reason why men followed men like him - money. *So, where was the money coming from? Not farms like Maria's that's for sure.* He also knew what Maria was saying about thousands of men dying was true. John didn't know the area well, but he knew there was thick jungle that stretched for hundreds of miles, and Kabila and his men would be well bedded in by now - it would be like pulling a cobra out of its shelter with your bear hands - you would get bitten.

John was sure Maria would know why Joseph Kabila had decided to take over the land in that part of the Congo but decided to change the conversation; he could see how upset it had made her. But before he could speak, she'd asked him a question, a question he'd heard so many times before and each time tried to avoid answering.

'Are you really just a journalist, John?'

He knew he couldn't answer her with the truth; it would put his life in danger, and possibly hers too. 'Yes, of course, I'm just a journalist.' He always answered the question in this way because it wasn't a lie, but what he'd done before being a journalist was a whole other story.

The Journalists - Congo Rescue

Maria was sure he wasn't just a journalist but could see he didn't want to say, this was fine by her, it was his business. But as far as she was concerned, he was an angel, an avenging angel sent to help the weak and the vulnerable. She'd never met anyone like John and now was glad she'd skidded off the track. 'Well, I think you're an angel, John.'

John laughed, though not actually sure how serious she was. 'Oh, that does smell good.'

'Of course it does, my grandmother's the best cook in the whole world.'

Maria noticed her grandmother waving them over.

'It's ready John. Let's go eat.'

'Gladly.' John said, while rubbing his belly and licking his lips after taking a last sip of his coffee.

The table was huge and John hadn't seen such a display of food, not since he attended a wedding at the Hilton London. He felt a little guilty knowing that they really couldn't afford to lay on such a display, but after seeing their faces and their smiles, he wasn't about to spoil things now. Even young Gia had a look of shock on his face; they obviously hadn't gone to so much trouble in a long time, if ever. Maria's grandmother sat at the head of the table with a smile so wide and revealing what teeth she had left. John knew this must be special for her too, all the family looking so happy, and knowing that they were not going to be harassed by Amos and his friends ever again.

Maria didn't want this time to end, and she didn't want John to finish his meal because she knew once he had he would leave. She hadn't been this happy in such a long time, but she knew it had to end and she knew she had to be strong. She knew that John was only here to do a job and that he had to continue his journey to Goma.

After their meal, John was sitting back in the armchair with a full stomach. He was watching Maria's nephews wash down his car and removing the mud he'd collected on the track from Kinshasa. It was also going to be hard for him to leave after being treated so kindly by Maria's family. He'd become more than a little attached to them all, especially Maria and Gia. She was a beautiful young woman in every which way and he knew she would be in his heart for quite some time. Although he knew at the same time he had a job to do, and that job wasn't just in the Congo, it was a job that took him all around the world, a job that led to the most dangerous places on the planet, a job he sometimes swore about, and a job that kept him single, but it was a job he knew he loved.

'So, what will you do with all these bodies,' John asks Maria as she approached him on the porch.

'Ah, well, once you have gone, John, we'll call the police, they will ask a few questions, and there will be no mention of you. They don't need to know you even exist. Then, they will load the bodies up on their truck and take them away to be cremated. No one is going to miss these guys I can assure you, and the police will probably be grateful they're dead.'

'Oh, right, well, that sounds good to me,' John said, smiling. 'I'm afraid that time has come, Maria, I must go. Thank you all, it's been a pleasure being here,' John said, but did not find that easy.

Maria's head dropped, she knew this moment was coming, but it didn't make it any easier. 'It's okay John, I understand, let me walk you to your car.'

'Of course,' John said, while giving Maria a peck on the cheek.

As they walked towards the car, young Gia run towards John at great speed and with tears running down his face. John picked him up and carried him towards the car. 'He's a great chap I'm going to miss him, I'm going to miss you all,' John said, while passing Gia to Maria.

The Journalists - Congo Rescue

'He's going to miss you too, John, I'm going to miss you.'

John knew stringing out this goodbye was only going to make it worse. He opened the door to his vehicle and after putting his small bag on the passenger seat, he got in. He started the engine and pulled away with one arm out of the window to wave goodbye.

As he drove up the small track he looked into his rearview-mirror and could see the whole family standing there and waving. John felt sad, but also happy that he'd made their lives just that little more bearable.

On that thought Joseph Kabila entered his head. He was a man that he'd only heard about, but he was a man that he hated with every beat of his heart. He was a man that had taken land from people who had worked hard all their lives to own, to watch it flourish, only to see it being taken away from them by ruthless murderers who hadn't done a hard day's work in their lives. John knew he would have to find out more about this Joseph Kabila.

--*Chapter Seven*--

IT WAS AROUND three in the afternoon by the time John had finally reached Goma. On his way he'd seen two dead bodies that paved the roadside. People passed them like they might a stray dog. He'd known that he was close to Goma. Now he was driving down the dust filled street that should lead him to a familiar sight. It was filled with pedestrians, walking and cycling, some had motorbikes. There were very few cars; people here couldn't afford such luxury, just the odd truck was parked at the side of the road delivering goods. John was sure once they'd delivered their load they'd be returning to where ever they had come from, rather than spend a night here. Originally it was John's plan too, to visit the hospital and head straight back to Kinshasa, but everything had changed and now he knew he would have to spend the night there.

John spotted four rebels walking along the side of the road as though they owned the place. Strings of ammo hung from their shoulders, their AK-47s swinging in the grip of their hands. They were lean and muscular, and the civilians were giving them a wide berth. He knew this was a common sight here in Goma, even though there was now a testimonial government whom were doing their best to rain in the rebels. But not here, there was no law here, no police, no government troops, not since the war ended, and the few government officials there were, were corrupt. Even God had forgotten this place.

John finally spotted the familiar sight he'd been looking for - the Goma Residence. It was a hotel that he'd stayed at before, and he knew it was at least clean. He parked up in front of the hotel, grabbed his bag and exited the vehicle. He wanted to check in quickly, have a shower and head straight to the hospital before it got dark. His plan was to leave this place early in the morning and head back to Kinshasa; he didn't want to stay here more than one night.

The front of the hotel was covered in dust from the road, and, well, it had to be said, it looked like a real shit hole.

He swung the door open knowing that unless there was new management the inside shouldn't look half bad. To his relief it hadn't changed a bit, right down to the fact there were very few people that actually stayed there. To his left was a small seating area where a couple of western tourist's sat on the quite plush PVC armchairs. They reminded him of Maria. *Maybe she'll take them to see the Volcano, or maybe even the mass graves,* he chuckled under his breath. To his right there was another small seating area and there he'd seen something that had stopped him in his tracks. He'd spotted a man sitting there wearing a white trilby with a black two inch band around it. Actually, it was more like cream in colour, smoke stained, with the odd small hole in it, a hat that could belong to only one person - Harry Smith.

'Harry, is that you?' John asks, while still not quite believing it.

Harry looked up in amazement. 'Well, knock me down with a feather. John is that really you, how long has it been, two, three years.' The look on Harry's face was of pure delight.

'Closer to three, I believe.' John said, before shaking the hand of his very good friend.

'Please, join me,' Harry insisted while pointing at the chair that stood the other side of a small table.

'Of course, my old friend,' John said, sincerely wanting to catch up, but not forgetting his plans.

'Hey, less of the old, pal, well, maybe a little old, hey,' Harry chuckled. 'Join me in a drink, John?' Harry had a small bottle of Jonnie Walker sat on the small table, he hadn't purchased it at the hotel, they didn't sell alcohol. But Harry had his contacts; where ever he went he had his contacts. He was a journalist, but unlike John he was self employed, which meant he had to pay for everything. But he was also an excellent wheeler dealer and had his paws in everything; he needed to have, just to cover his expenses.

'Well, just a small one then, it is the real thing. right?' John said jokingly, but actually knew better, he knew Harry well, and he knew he could purchase things that no other man could. John knew he wouldn't be drinking it if it wasn't the real thing.

'You know better than that, my friend, right.'

'Of course, Harry, just joking, pal.' John could see his plans going to shit in front of his eyes as Harry poured his drink, but he hadn't seen Harry in nearly three years and he really wanted to catch up, he really wanted to know what he'd been up to. 'Last I heard you were in the Sudan, you met Chris there, right.'

'Yes, that's right, it was great to see him. If I remember correctly, he'd just rescued a young girl from a Janjaweed leader, it was the main story for weeks after that, but no one had the slightest clue who done it.

'That would be about right. Chris wouldn't have left any clues.' John felt a sense of pride just talking about his colleague.

'Actually, I gave him a story; it was too dangerous for me to follow it.'

'Ah, you mean the weapons smuggling into Chad.'

'That's right.'

'Well, Chris destroyed the lot.'

'He did, but what about the story.'

'He didn't care; he was more concerned about where the weapons were going, and whose hands they might fall into.'

'Um, always the hero. You too, John.'

The Journalists - Congo Rescue

'Yeah, well, sometimes lives are more important than the story, Harry,' John said, while emptying his glass. 'That's some good whisky, Harry.'

'Would you like some more?'

John could see the small bottle was empty. 'Yes, but . . .'

'Don't worry. I'll soon take care of that.' Harry took his phone out of his cream coloured jacket pocket and dialed a number. He spoke in the local dialogue, he was clever like that. 'It will be here in just a second,' Harry said, while waving at the hotel porter. Within seconds a young Congolese man entered the hotel with another small bottle of whiskey wrapped in a piece of cloth. Harry slipped him his payment and the young man disappeared as quickly as he'd shown up. A second later the hotel porter had turned up with a small bucket of ice and two small bottles of soda.

John sat there in astonishment, he knew how Harry worked, but it still never failed to amaze him. 'Well, that's how it's done, right, Harry.'

Harry smiled. 'Yes, that's how it's done my friend, one cube or two,' Harry asked, after pouring the whisky.

Normally John would go without the ice, knowing where the water might have come from, but not this time, this time he knew it would be fine. 'Two's fine Harry.'

John knew that Harry had contacts all over the African continent and also in the Middle East. He had contacts that would give him stories that otherwise no westerner would hear about. He had contacts that would sell him gems, and contacts that would steal for him, for example if he needed a vehicle. He was known all over the region, though there were some countries where he had outstayed his welcome. He'd been known to bribe officials to get information about corruption within the government; once these stories were printed he had to stay clear. It wasn't a problem, at least not yet. He travelled a lot, going from one country to the next, knowing when to move on was the secret, and Harry was an expert.

'So, John, what is it you're reporting on.'

'Oh, I'm here to report on the Aids pandemic.'

'Ah, nasty business is that, I couldn't do that, going into those hospitals seeing all those poor blighters suffering like that.'

John understood, he'd seen the sights, and it was still playing on his mind. 'It's terrible, Harry, even I struggled.'

The Journalists - Congo Rescue

'You, you must have seen worse than that, I'm guessing there's nothing you haven't seen throughout your career.'

'Well, you're right, of course, and it surprised me too, but it's the knowing that these people are innocent of any kind of atrocity, just families already trying to make life worth living. It's not like seeing murdering rebels, or terrorists dying.'

'Um, I can see what you mean, John. John something happened this morning and I've been trying not to tell you because I know what you'll probably do.'

John was curious, but not sure if he even wanted to know. Just looking at Harry's face, he could see it was important. 'Go on Harry, what is it?' John said, while taking a large sip of his whisky.

'A group of five tourists, they were just walking down the street when two trucks pulled up full of rebels, they grabbed the tourists apparently kicking and screaming, and threw them into the back of their trucks.'

John cringed at the thought of it, and dreaded what might happen to them. But on that rare occasion had decided that they would have known the dangers and if they were willing to take the risk, they would have to accept the consequences.

'That's terrible Harry, poor bastards,' John said, before taking another sip - he was really enjoying the whisky, and the company.

Harry was a little surprised; the John he remembered would have already been trying to find out stuff, trying to find out where the rebels would have taken them. But Harry was glad, he didn't want John going on this mission; he knew it would be too dangerous, even for him. 'So you're not going after them, that's good, I'm glad.'

'Well, I can't rescue everyone, Harry. If they want to come to these sorts of places, then, well, it's up to them.'

'Good on you, John, bloody South American twits.'

'What!' John said, nearly choking on his whiskey.

'Apparently, they were South American, there were for men and a beautiful Latino woman, god only knows what those rebels will do to her.'

'Oh, shit,' John said, under his breath after realising he knew the group he was talking about.

'You okay, John, you look as though you might know who I'm talking about,' Harry saw the look on John's face after he'd mentioned they were South American. Harry had seen this look on John's face before.

The Journalists - Congo Rescue

'Yeah, I met the woman in Kinshasa; they were here to see the Gorillas.'

'Well, the only gorillas they'll see now are the type that carry ammo over their shoulders, wield an AK-47, and an eighteen inch machete,' Harry said, but could see John was taking it all a little more seriously. 'How well did you actually know this woman, John?'

'Not that well, not really, though I did spend the night with her,' John said, while remembering the night of passion they'd shared.

'Well, I'd say that meant you knew her quite well then.' Harry could see John was deep in thought, so he remained quiet for a moment.

'Harry,' John said, while rubbing his chin. 'How well do you know the Shaba area?'

Harry was beginning to wish he hadn't said anything. He had an idea why John was interested in the Shaba area. 'Not that well, I have visited the area, it's very pretty, has nice farms, and mountains in the surrounding areas.'

'That doesn't sound like the sort of place you'd visit, Harry.'

'That's right, but I had to meet a chap up there, he had some gems he wanted to sell, diamonds, and rubies, very cheap too,' Harry said, while rubbing his hands and looking quite proud of himself.

'Why Shaba, is that area rich in minerals.' John's mind was working overtime; he'd been trying to understand why Joseph Kabila was so interested in the area.

'Absolutely, I've purchased plenty of gems there; gems that the miners had managed to smuggle out and needed to sell in a hurry, all uncut of course, but I know people who are interested in uncut diamonds, I could usually move them quite quickly. But that all stopped when Kabila took over the area. The few miners that did manage to smuggle out any diamonds were rounded up and shot.'

'So, that's it then,' John said to himself, though loud enough for Harry to hear.

'What's it, John?'

'Ah, well, I've been trying to figure out where Kamila is getting his money from, but now it's clear enough.'

'Ah, the diamonds you mean, um, but that wouldn't be enough, John.'

John raised his eyebrows at Harry unsure of what he was trying to say.

Harry could tell John was confused. 'Having the diamonds is one thing, selling them is another thing. We're talking about billions, and there's no one in the Congo that has that kind of money, and even if there was, the government would come down on them hard, no one is allowed to purchase diamonds from Kabila.'

John pondered on it for a while; he knew what Harry was saying made all the sense in the world. He was sure there must be a third party and that third party was not Congolese. He was getting the diamonds out of the country; the big question was, how.

'Harry, the rebels that took the group, I'm assuming they were Kabila's rebels, right.' John had to wonder with them being so far from their stronghold.

'It's not exactly my forte, rebel groups, John.'

'No, of course not, Harry, sorry.'

'But the answer to your question is, yes, because all the other rebel groups got concessions from the new government, positions in power, land, this kind of thing. But Kabila was deemed to be too violent. He'd crossed the Zaire River and destroyed a village, raping the women before burning them alive, the men and children had also died a terrible death. Some say he's insane; there was no reason at all for him to cross the river, the republic of Congo was not part of the war.'

'Um, so now he's building an army and planning to take over the new government I guess.'

'Possibly, who knows what a man like that is capable of, one thing's for sure, it doesn't bare thinking about - but surely you're not considering going down to Shaba, John?' Harry asked, while lifting his hat and scratching his head, and while showing what little white hair he had left.

'I was considering it Harry, but I think this one would be beyond my capability. I don't even know the area. I could be searching the Jungle for weeks and not even see a single rebel.'

'That's not to mention you'd be out numbered, about three thousand to one.' Harry added.

'That wouldn't necessarily be a problem; it would be a rescue mission and the fewer of us the better. But you're right Harry, going it alone, not knowing the area, would be suicide.' But that didn't take away the fact he was worried about Martina, the beautiful Latino woman who came to his room for one reason only -to have sex.

'Well, now that's all out of the way, let's enjoy the rest of this whisky, after all, as you know it's not easy to come by,' Harry said, under a small chuckle, and a wink.

'Alright, pour us another one, Harry.'

The Journalists - Congo Rescue

It was almost six o'clock in the evening before Harry had to go and meet a guy regarding a story. He and John had chatted for ages and finished a third small bottle of whiskey. Now, after finally checking into the hotel John was in his room taking a shower. He held his head under the shower head, the water was at a decent pressure, and the temperature was almost perfect, a very rare thing in Africa, let alone in the Congo. He was standing there while the warm, almost hot water ran over his head and over his ears, dulling any sound if only slightly.

Something was rattling away in his head and he was trying to make sense of it. The fact he and Harry had gotten through three small bottles of whiskey wasn't helping, but the water running over his head was. He was trying to figure out exactly why the rebels had taken the South American group. Kidnappings were not rare in the Congo; it was a means of making money and John knew that many ransoms had been paid. But there was something else, the fact that Martina's family were in the jewellery business, and Kabila had taken over an area that was rich in minerals. John felt there must be some kind of connection. He rattled his brain for what seemed like ages, but he just couldn't quite make the connection.

The Journalists - Congo Rescue

John sat on his bed hurting and feeling very frustrated. He'd become quite fond of Martina in the short time they'd spent together. However, he knew if he never saw her again he'd soon forget her, but this was different, just thinking about what those rebels might do to her was ripping at his heart, and the fact that he couldn't do anything was just making things worse. But he knew no man in his right mind would go searching in a jungle that was full of rebels and covered an area as big as the UK.

--Chapter Eight--

JOHN HADN'T HAD a good night's sleep, and it was because of what Harry had said about Martina's group screaming and kicking as they were being loaded onto the rebels trucks that had done it, it had rattled around in his head all night. But as he glanced over to the window the sun was tempting him, luring him to go take a look. He climbed out of bed, and just wearing his underpants he approached the window. The view was magnificent; the Congo was a beautiful place despite its endless troubles. In the distance he could see the Congo River snake its way through the endless lush green vegetation, beyond that mountains displayed a beautiful sunrise.

The wildlife thrived in the Congo, mainly because the Congolese people had been too busy killing each other to worry about catching rare animal species that they could have sold for top dollar. In John's opinion, this is what made the Congo Basin so special. Birds in their millions were singing their morning songs, and monkeys could be heard making their mating calls in the distance. He knew this would probably not last now that the war was over so he relished the moment, closing his eyes and just listening.

However, the beautiful sounds were soon disrupted by a tap on the door. John refused to open his eyes even to the sound of someone knocking on his door. He knew it wasn't room service, because there was no room service. Then the knocking became slightly louder, John had no option, he had to answer it.

He wiggled himself into his khakis, but felt there was no need to put on a shirt before answering it. He opened it with some reluctance, though, while also being full of curiosity. To his amazement there were two soldiers standing there, though John saw them as probably guards, maybe from a consulate or something similar. Their skin was tanned and there uniform looked familiar, but John couldn't quite put a country to them. 'Can I help you gents?'

'John Stone?' The younger of the two asks.

John guessed he was only about eighteen, and had reminded him of *his* first months in the forces. He was unsure as to why they knew his name, but did have his suspicions. 'Why, who's asking.'

'Sir, we'd like you to accompany us to the Brazilian-Embassy.'

Telling them to take a hike had crossed his mind, but once they'd mentioned the Brazilian Embassy John's mind had gone into overdrive. He now had to know what the Brazilian Embassy wanted with him, and did it have anything to do with Martina's group. 'Okay, could you wait for me in the reception area, please - I'd like to take a shower first.'

'Yes, Sir!' They said, before giving John a salute.

'There's no need for that guy's, it's been some time since I was in the forces.'

'Yes Sir!' they said again, only this time with like a half-salute, before they disappeared down the corridor.

The Journalists - Congo Rescue

John slipped out of his khakis again with a grin on his face. He'd actually enjoyed the moment, young soldiers showing their respect for the work he'd done, it had made him feel proud.

John took a quick shower; he didn't want to keep the young soldiers waiting in the reception area for too long. He could remember when he was their age, having to wait in civilian locations while dressed in full military attire. People would stare at him, take the mickey out of him, and even throw small things at him. It wasn't everyone who respected what he was and what he did.

John arrived at the reception area to see the two soldiers standing to attention just by the door, he could tell they were well trained and well disciplined. He himself might have taken advantage of the comfy looking PVC armchairs. At least there were no civilians other than a guy sat behind the reception desk with his head lying on the counter sound asleep.

'Come on, men, let's get out of here.' John said, while heading straight for the door.

'Yes, sir.'

A large black Benz was parked in front of John's vehicle; it had dark tinted windows and a small Brazilian flag standing proudly on the passenger side front wing.

The Journalists - Congo Rescue

'Sir.' One of the soldiers said as he opened the rear door.

'Thank you,' John said, almost feeling like royalty. He was almost tempted to ask the young soldiers what this was all about, but was sure they probably didn't know, and if they did, would probably be under orders not to say.

They soon arrived at some tall, iron double gates that were secured by a tall wall with iron spikes easily visible at the top. It was a sight that John had seen only too often since becoming a journalist and he knew it was something he had to address. The gates opened to reveal two more young guards pulling at the heavy gates to open them. The driver, a Congolese man, then drove into a small parking area. John's door was then opened by one of the other soldiers who led him into the building.

'This way, please, sir.'

John couldn't remember being called sir, so many times in such a small amount of time, but he didn't mind, actually he liked it.

The guard opened two large mahogany doors which led into a lash office. John could see a man who he assumed must be consular official sitting at a large desk directly in front of him, although probably seven meters away. John walked towards the desk, though slowly, he was taking in the beautiful office. In the corner was a seating area that consisted of a large brown leather sofa with gold rivet studs that held the well padded interior intact and there were two arm chairs to match. John guessed that was where the consular official would convene with the Congolese officials.

The walls were full of pictures that were all of Brazil, and as to be expected were all very colourful. Mainly the pictures were of the famous carnival, the Carnaval do Rio de Janeiro. Beautiful Brazilian women wearing dresses that had every colour you could think of. There were also pictures of the Amazon, with the Amazon River snaking its way through the never ending rain forest. Or at least this was what these pictures portrayed. John knew better, he knew that large areas of the Amazon rain forest were being cut down, making way for farmland and cattle grazing. He sighed as he approached the consular official's desk.

'Ah, Mr. John Stone, welcome.' The rather large if not intimidating man said, while reaching out his hand to John.

John shook his hand before sitting down in front of the official's desk. 'So, what's this about,' John asked, with a shrug.

The Journalists - Congo Rescue

The official was a little taken aback, he knew he towered over John's five-eleven stature by about four inches, and his chest size was twice that of John's, and usually people did find him a little threatening. But it was clear John didn't. 'Well, um, the thing is some of our citizens have been kidnapped.'

'I heard.' John said, while eager to know more, but not wanting to be too obvious. He also felt it better not to say too much, he wanted the consular to do the talking, that way he was hoping he might give away more than what he might have if he was doing the talking.

'You have, oh, well, then, you can understand my concern.'

John remained quiet, while giving a small nod.

'Anyway, in these situation's we contact governments from all over the world to try and find the most suitable man or men to lead a rescue mission, a man that is already in the Democratic Republic of Congo, or somewhere close by, someone who has experience in jungle warfare, and someone who has conducted this kind of mission before. Your name was at the top of the list.'

'Um, that happens a lot,' John said, while thinking this was something he needed to address soon. 'What do you know about who has taken them?'

'It's clear who's taken them, they were taken in broad daylight and there were hundreds of witnesses. It was this, Kabila guy.'

'Joseph Kabila, you mean.' John was amazed that the official could hardly remember his name. John hadn't taken to the Brazilian; there was something not quite right about him.

'Yes, that's him.' The consular official wasn't feeling comfortable talking to John; he was hoping he was going to be friendlier, more obedient. More of a yes sir, three bags full sir, kind of guy - he wasn't.

'Okay, you want me to lead a rescue mission, so who am I supposed to be leading and to where.' John didn't mix his words, he needed to know everything that this official knew, and so far he was not impressed.

'Come.' The official said, his arm stretched and pointing towards a small door at the left of the office.

John followed the official into another small office. At the centre of this office was a large oval shaped table, and on that John had noticed a map. There were two men studying the map, at least until John and the official had entered. John had also noticed someone dressed in full camouflage attire, sitting in the corner with his cap low over his face. He was black, so John assumed he must be Congolese.

'These men will be going with you, that is, of course if you agree to the mission.' One of the men turned away from the map to face John. This is Carlos Oliveira,' the Official said. The other man then turned too. 'And this is Jose Ramos. They are both trained in Jungle warfare, and have spent considerable time in our own Amazon jungle.'

John felt they looked more like hunters than military, nothing about this felt right. He approached the table and looked down at the map. He noticed where they had drawn a circle. 'Is this the location where you think the group is being held?'

'Yes, we believe so, if not, it's somewhere close,' the official said.

'If not, it's somewhere close!' John repeated, while shaking his head. 'Let's just get a few things clear, this is not the Amazon Jungle, you don't have just snakes and spiders to worry about.' John said, while looking at the two men. 'This is the Congo Basin, and it's full of rebel fighters who will cut you into small pieces without blinking an eye. Most of these rebels would have spent most of their lives living in the jungle, its home to them. The only chance we have of a successful mission is if we know exactly where the location is.'

The two men swallowed deeply.

'I know where it is,' the man sat in the corner said, in a strangely high voice.

'Ah, this is our guide; she knows the area very well.'

The woman who John had assumed was a man stood up and lifted her cap. It was difficult to put an age to her due to her face being full of scars. John guessed she was not that old, and probably at one time quite attractive. She approached the table and looked at the map closely. 'This area here is waterfall creek, there are hundreds of small waterfalls in this area and they all lead to this lake. This is where the main camp is, this is where you'll find your people.'

'Excuse me,' John said, in his politest tone. 'Do you mind if I ask your name?'

She liked John's face and felt sure he was a good man. She had also been listening to him, and she was sure he knew what he was doing. She hadn't gotten the same feeling from the other two men, whom she also was wary of. 'My name's Kapia.'

The Journalists - Congo Rescue

'Kapia, that's a nice name.' John paused for a second. 'Kapia, why is it you know so much, you've been here, right?' Kapia stared at John; it was a stare that was familiar to John, a stare full of pain and anger. John knew she'd suffered more pain and grief than anyone should ever suffer.

'I was held captive there for five years.'

John was sure she had so much more to say, but didn't want to put her through all of that. It was obvious enough that she knew the location, and John knew she had her own reasons for wanting to go back, but this was reason for concern, and John knew he would have to confront her about it sooner rather later.

'Okay then, I'll arrange some four wheel vehicles to take you there,' the official said, while feeling confident that it was a go.

'No, you can't travel by road to this location. You have to travel by boat up the Congo River.'

'But that would take days,' Carlos said.

Kapia pointed at the map again. 'If we travel by road, this point is as close as you'll get to the location. It's a twenty mile track through dense jungle. You'll need machetes just to cut a path through it. It could take weeks. There is a single track made by the rebel's, but even if we were to find it, it's constantly used by them. By boat we can reach this point in three maybe four days, it's only four miles from the location.'

John knew that Kapia's way was the only way, but he also knew the point she'd pointed to on the map would also be swarming with rebels. 'What's this point here?' he asked, pointing to a place further back down the river.

'Ah, this is a place that the rebels never use, it's swampland which stretches for around two miles.'

John felt that this was an area that Kapia was familiar with. 'Can it be past, Kapia?'

'This was how I escaped, yes, it can be past, but it's full of crocodiles and snakes, and we will have to wade through swamp water up to our waists, yes, I think this is best.'

'Surly there's a better route than this,' Jose said, with a look that clearly showed he was not keen.

'Not if you want to rescue your citizens and live to tell the tale.' John said, with a firm tone.

John could only imagine how desperate Kapia must have been to escape via this route. But was it fear for her life, or determination to live to fight another day. The fact she was going back had him curious.

The Journalists - Congo Rescue

Carlos and Jose both looked at the official, it was clear they weren't too pleased with the plan, which had gotten John even more curious as to what exactly their plan was.

'There is just one problem with this plan,' the official said. 'Where are we supposed to get a boat from?'

John looked at Kapia, she just shrugged.

'Well, that's just perfect,' Carlos said, with a look that indicated he was just that little bit pleased.

'Let me just make a call,' John said.

Carlos's face dropped.

John took his phone out of his pocket, and dialed a number. 'Harry, I need your help with something.'

'Hi John, anything pal, what is it?'

'I need a boat and someone to pilot it. It has to be large enough to accommodate nine people, plus the pilot.'

'Oh, John, does this mean what I think it means?'

'Yes, I suspect it does, pal. Can you help?'

'Um, sorry, John, I don't have a boat.'

John sighs.

Carlos grins after seeing John sigh.

'But I do know someone that can steal one for me, John.'

John grins.

Carlos sighs.

'We need it first thing, Harry.'

'No problem, I will give you the location tonight at the hotel.'

'Okay, Harry, cheers pal.'

'Who's Harry,' the official asks with a slight look of surprise, and not thinking John would know anyone in the Congo. He'd done his research; he knew John was here to report on the Aids pandemic and that now he was just a Journalist. His name had popped up at the top of the list, but this was only part of the reason he'd chosen him.

'Harry...let's just say he's a man of means, and a good friend,' John didn't feel the need to say anymore than that. 'Right, there's just one more thing we're going to need - weapons.'

'That's not a problem, we have plenty of weapons.'

'Okay, great, so as soon as I know where the boat will be moored I'll contact you. It will be early, around 4.00 am, so get some sleep. For the next week or so you probably won't get much.'

John was still wary about the mission, and couldn't quite understand why he was going. It for sure played on his mind, those five civilians being held in conditions that he was sure they were not used to, probably placed in bamboo cages, no bigger than one metre high, unable to stretch, unable to sleep. Mosquitoes sucking on their blood, fed leftovers by the rebel's while they danced by their fires. No person should be put through such hell, to suffer this way. John knew if anyone could rescue them it was him, he couldn't just leave them there, that weren't the kind of man he was.

John looked at the Consular official indicating that he'd like a word in private. The official led him back into the main office where he sat behind his desk while John sat in the same chair as before. John stared into the official's eyes and it was the Consular official who was feeling intimidated.

'Are you sure these men are up to the job, because like I said before, this is not the Amazon Jungle. If they're not, it would be better if you say now, before you get us all killed.'

'Do you know what a Favela is, John?'

John did know what a Favela was; it's a slum which is usually found on the outskirts of a big city. It was a place where people with very little income would build their own city or shanty where only the poor would live. But he also knew they were breeding grounds for drug dealers, murderers, and small time crooks. He knew the police seldom entered the compact areas, where snipers would aim their rifles out of small windows and never be seen. He knew the police who worked in these areas had to be highly trained to enter homes where even the kids had guns. 'Yes, I know what a Favela is.'

'Well, these men have been patrolling these places for the last three years, sometimes having to chase drug dealers into the Amazon. So you see, there aren't just snakes and spiders to worry about. Also, before this, these two men were in our Special Forces, and have conducted rescue missions not too un-similar to this one. Rich kids are often kidnapped in Brazil, and these two men have rescued dozens.'

John was feeling a little better for their chat. At least now he knew he'd be going into the Jungle with people who can handle themselves, but freeing children from a few kidnappers, couldn't compare to freeing a group of five from three thousand rebels. Now his only real concern was if they could take orders from someone they didn't know, and someone who wasn't South American. 'You know there can only be one man in charge, and that man has to be me,' John said, still staring into the consular officials eyes.

'Yes, absolutely, of course, John, I wouldn't have it any other way,' the official was beginning to wonder whether he'd made the wisest choice in choosing John. He'd already learned that he was not a man to mess with, and if things were to go wrong it could be his ass on the line.

'Okay, finally, there's a question of payment. I personally won't be requiring anything. I don't carry out these kinds of mission's for money. But clearly my friend Harry will require payment for the boat and for the pilot that I expect will be with us for anything up to two weeks.'

'Of course, John, just let me know where your friend is staying and I will personally make sure he's well looked after.'

'Well, he's staying at the same hotel as me, the Goma Residence room 349.' John then stood up. 'Okay, I'll call you as soon as I have a location.' He didn't shake the official's hand again; he didn't like him enough for that. He just left the Office without saying anything else.

The Official was left wiping his brow; he'd never met anyone like John before and had never felt so intimidated by a man who was much smaller than him. He prayed to himself sincerely hoping that he never has to meet him again, at least not after he'd seen them off and watched them head up the Congo River.

--Chapter Nine--

THAT EVENING JOHN was sitting in his room and going over the mission in his head, he was trying to cover every possible scenario. It was something he always did, but he knew this was no ordinary mission. It was without doubt the most dangerous mission, he'd ever planned. You might even call it foolhardy, or reckless. Every possibility had to be considered, even them being caught by Joseph Kabila's rebels, was not off the table.

Suddenly, but not unexpected, there was a familiar tap on the door. John grinned. He knew exactly who it was and was now looking forward to meeting with him again. 'Hello, Harry, good to see you again, pal.'

Harry entered with a swift lift of his hat. 'Hi John, you crazy bustard,' Harry said, grinning, but with real concern flowing through his veins, especially as it was him who had mentioned the South Americans being taken. He knew he didn't need to annoy John with stupid questions like, are you sure you want to do this, or, do you realise how dangerous this is. He knew if John didn't think it was possible he wouldn't be doing it, and he also knew trying to change his mind now would be like telling him not to jump after he already had - impossible.

'Alright, I'm guessing you managed to locate a boat for us, Harry?'

'Yes, of course, John. It's a little shabby looking, but my man assures me the engine is virtually new. It's large enough to house nine people comfortably and well, I've added a little something at the stern.'

'You have, what is it, Harry?'

'Ah, you'll see, let's just say it should help you if you're being chased by those blood thirsty rebels.'

John really wanted to know what it was, but could see Harry wanted it to be a surprise. 'Okay, Harry, thanks anyhow.'

'Oh, and the pilot, she knows the river well and apparently had to flee the area too, because of Joseph Kabila.

'She, Harry?'

'Yes, she's a woman John, and not too hard on the eyes I must say.'

'Oh, Harry, this is not a vacation we're going on, and I for sure don't need any distractions.'

'Um, sorry John, I wasn't thinking, I'll try and find someone else, though she really needed the work, poor girl.'

John recognised the disappointed look on Harry's face. 'You say she knows the river well?'

'Yes, she's been travelling up and down it all of her life.'

'And you say she knows the area?'

'She lived there; her family had a farm there, just like I said, until Joseph, bloody, Kabila took over the area. That bastard, he's ruined so many lives, and just because he's pissed with the government. John, I know this mission is not to kill him, but I must say, the sooner he dies the happier I will be.'

The Journalists - Congo Rescue

'You and thousands more, Harry, you and thousands more.'

John suddenly found himself thinking about Maria. It was Harry mentioning the pilot having to flee the area too that did it. It had just reminded him how much he was missing her and her family. He wasn't sure whether he loved Maria, not really loved her, but he knew if she was to walk into his room right now, he'd give her one hell of a hug.

Harry hadn't mentioned anything about payment and John was sure he probably wouldn't. 'Oh, regarding your payment Harry, I assume they'll deliver it to you here, the consular did ask where you were staying.'

'Oh, that's fine, don't give it a second thought, you have enough on your plate as it is. Personally, I think you must be a little mad, but that's just because I know I wouldn't dare.' Harry lifted his hat and gave his head a little scratch. 'But really, you and Chris must be the bravest people on the planet, I know what you've both achieved, the people you've rescued, and that's with no Intel, that you would otherwise of had if you were still in the forces,' Harry said, while almost becoming emotional.

'Thanks Harry, that means a lot.'

'Well, I think you both deserve the Nobel Prize, or at least a medal.'

John just sat there with a smile on his face, a smile that was full of gratitude. He also knew there might not have been a mission if not for Harry and his unique way of getting things. 'So are you planning to remain in Goma for a while?'

'A few more days, I think. I'm waiting for a guy who says he has two original spears from way back then; those things are worth an absolute fortune, and I've already located a buyer in South Africa.'

'Wow, Harry, those things are worth a fortune. Well, I hope you make a killing, and maybe make enough to retire back home in the UK, and live the rest of your life relaxing with your feet up.'

'Oh, John, what a horrible thought, that's not me at all.'

John knew he wasn't, no more than it was him, but he'd still like to see it, just to know he's safe. 'I know that's not you Harry, but you do live on the edge a little; it would just be nice to know you're safe, that's all.'

'Huh, it's the living on the edge that keeps me alive, John. Huh, talking about living on the edge.'

John smiled. 'Fair comment, Harry. Speaking of that I'd better get some rest, I have an early start and I need to contact the Consular Official, to give him the location of the boat.'

Harry stood up. 'Yes, of course you do John,' He said, while reaching a hand out to John.

They shook hands and even gave each other a small hug. Harry had wanted to ask so much about the mission, and he wanted to know who would be joining him on the rescue. He'd done dealings with South American people before, and in his experience they weren't the most trustworthy people. But he knew John had to get his rest, he knew for the next week at least, he would need to be fully alert. Harry wasn't so worried for the South Americans, he knew in John they had the best man there was to conduct their rescue. He was a man who had rescued dozens of people throughout his time in the forces, and almost as many since being a journalist. He knew that some of the missions that John had completed had been seen as impossible, and even described as suicide missions. But each time he had succeeded, and each time had had no desire for any payment at all. Harry knew he wasn't just the bravest man he knew, he was also the best man he knew.

*

John's early morning call was bang on time, and the first thing that had entered his mind was what he was about to undertake. This was a good thing, because he knew this would be all that mattered in the coming days and maybe weeks. He knew what he was about to undertake was probably going to be his biggest challenge yet, and he knew it might even be a challenge to far. But fear was something that John had been trained to ignore. He knew it only distracted a person, which was something he couldn't allow.

Having only two sets of clothes he was pleased to see that they had been washed and stood just outside his door. After taking a shower and getting dressed, John took one last glance at the room, knowing full well that it would be the last thing he saw for a while, that even resembled comfort.

He was hit with the normal blanket of humidity while exiting the hotel, even though it was only four am. But he knew where he was heading the humidity would get far worse, especially deep in the jungle. A place where mosquitoes thrived along with the deceases they carried.

Before long, he was driving up a small dirt track to where his good friend Harry had said the boat was moored. There was no port in Goma, not even a small docking area. The river was just a branch that leads off the main river and was only about eight metres wide.

As John arrived at the location he could see that everyone was already there. A Landrover discovery was parked close to the boat where he could see the South Americans off loading their equipment, which was mainly food, water, and weapons.

'Good morning gents,' John said, while wanting to at least start the trip in a friendly atmosphere.

'Good morning,' Carlos Oliveira said, but not too convincingly.

Jose Ramos just nodded his head.

Good morning, John,' Kapia said, with a smile that had made her face crease up in an unusual way.

John was sure it was because of all the scars on the poor woman's face.

John assessed the weapons first - there was a good collection.

'I hope these will be suffice?' A voice said from behind where John was standing.

John turned to see it was the Consular Official, who was dressed as though he was about to go to dinner at the Savoy, his gold watch hanging on his wrist as if it was too heavy to just rest there. His hair was greased back over his ears - not a single hair was out of place. John felt like telling him he was a little overdressed for such an occasion.

'Yes, these should do,' John said, while looking down and reaching for an AK-47 in which there were plenty. He'd also noticed there were box's of magazines, grenades, pistols, a good selection of knives and other weapons that were still concealed in there box's. 'Hopefully we won't need any of these, but it's always better to be prepared, don't you think.'

'In what possible scenario would you not need weapons, John?' The official said, with a look of shock if not surprise at what John had just said.

John could see he was confused 'Alright, everyone gather round please. You too, Kapia if you would.'

The three of them walked over to where John and the official stood. 'Okay, we are well armed,' John said, pointing at the weapons. 'And we all have a fair amount of experience in the horrors of warfare, including Kapia here.' John said, reaching an arm in her direction. She smiled because she appreciated him including her, even though her experience was at the other end of the knife. 'It won't make even the smallest difference, even if we were about to enter the jungle in armoured vehicles, fully dressed in bullet proof clothing, it would not make a difference. There are three thousand rebels, all well armed and all fearless. We are just four; they could cut us down before we even got the chance to start running.' John looked at the group, his face was serious. 'My point is, this is a rescue mission, and under no circumstances must we try to confront the rebels. We find the camp, we assess the camp for some time, and we sneak in, free the civilians, and sneak out.' John bent down and picked up one of the knives. 'God forbid this is the only weapon we will need. We have to be quiet, we have to be speedy, and we have to be brave.' John paused for a moment. 'Okay, that's all, and may god protect us.'

The official now knew John was a man who lived up to his reputation, and the fact his name had appeared at the top of the list was no accident. The main reason he'd chosen John was because he saw he was just a Journalist now, he thought maybe he'd forgotten his training. Now he was beginning to think that John Stone could actually pull it off. It had him worried, very worried. Feeling more than a little anxious he glanced over to his men before returning to his vehicle, getting in, and driving off.

John stood on the bank for a while just looking at the boat. As Harry had said, it was a little shabby looking. The quite large vessel was made of wood, which had been varnished but not for some time, so it was peeling in places, mainly the top half. The hull down to the water line looked fine; beneath this John had no idea. But it did have a roof where they could seek shelter from the sun, this was critical. Around ten metres long, John was sure it had travelled the Congo River for many years. The pilot had started the engine and it seemed to be ticking over nicely. John was impressed. He sincerely hoped he'd be able to return it in the same condition and return it to its owner. But for now it was their means of getting up the Congo River, it would take them to their destination, and more importantly, it would be their home.

'Okay, let's head off,' John called out, after removing the small mooring rope that had been tied around a tree, and climbing aboard the boat.

The pilot increased the revs, and the boat left its mooring's behind to start the long journey up the Congo River. John assessed the boat further and soon realised there would be very little comfort with just solid wood benches to sleep on, and very little space to stretch, especially once the boat was full. He was also sure there would be no complaints, not from the South American group. He could only imagine what they were having to endure.

The Journalists - Congo Rescue

About to sit down, and maybe take a nap, he remembered what Harry had said about putting something on the stern, something he wanted to be a surprise. In just a few strides he'd arrived at the stern to see nothing much at all, or at least nothing visible. There was for sure something that was mounted at the centre of the deck, and that looked a little out of place. It was covered by a plastic sheet that was tied firmly. As John untied the few knots that were holding the plastic sheet in place, an idea of what it might be entered into his mind. *No, no way, it couldn't be.* But it was. Standing proudly at the centre of the stern was a fifty calibre machine gun, standing on its own pedestal and loaded and ready to fire. John knew how difficult it must have been to acquire such a weapon, but then he did know who acquired it. *'Harry ,how do you do it?'* John knew only his friend Harry could have acquired such a weapon, and just as Harry had said; it would be very useful if they were being chased by a rebel boat.

John soon replaced the plastic sheet. He didn't want to attract attention, and he knew they'd be passing through several small towns before they headed deep into the jungle.

It was around an hour later when they finally reached the main river. John was a little astounded at just how wide it was at this point, but he had studied the river and knew it had its wide points as well as its narrow points. At this part of the river there were boats, both heading up river as well as heading down river. The boats heading down river were full to the brim, passengers sitting right on the edge where they could easily fall overboard. John was sure they would probably be heading to Kinshasa, leaving their rural homes to look for work, or to get supplies. A small flock of birds followed the boats that had the most people; it was as if they knew where the best pickings would be. They'd dive low to pick at the food waste as the passengers threw it overboard, sometimes catching it before it even reached the water.

There was a slight breeze that carried with it the smell of the river, a smell that John has always liked, even though it was a kind of dirty smell. He looked over the side to see that the tide was flowing down river, and explained why the boats heading down river seem to be travelling that much faster. The water was definitely dirty and littered with just about anything that floated.

It would be some hours before they passed the first town, which would be Mbandaka, in the Equateur Province; it's a place where the new government is establishing a new military base. The idea being, if the rebels were to come down river, they could stop them before they reached Kinshasa. But John knew that would never happen, he was sure that Joseph Kabila would have more sense than that. Why would he take his rebels from the security of the jungle to deliver them to the Government forces, it just wouldn't make sense. But to the Congolese people who knew nothing, it would look like the government is at least doing something.

This area was where the Congo River confluence with the Ruki Rivers and John was sure it would need an experienced pilot to navigate it. He decided it was probably a good a time as any to go meet her.

On his way to the bow, he noticed Carlos Oliveira, and Jose Ramos had found themselves a bench and was using their rucksack as a pillow. He couldn't actually blame them for that, it had been an early start, and he knew they would need to get all the rest they could before heading deep into the jungle. There, they will need to be on full alert, looking for rebel boats, and searching their eyes along the river bank, day and night. Kapia on the other hand had found herself a pistol, and had stripped it down for cleaning. John knew she would be a useful asset to this mission having spent time with the rebels, and living in the camp. He had already figured her to be the bravest woman he'd met, but he knew before they got close to their destination he would have to sit down with her and have a good chat.

'Good morning, skipper,' John said, as he approached the pilot from behind.

'Good morning, John,' she said, after turning around and looking at him.

John just stood there for a moment, eyes wide. 'Maria!'

--Chapter Ten--

Three days previous.

CHRIS WAS SITTING up straight, after the air-hostess had announced that they would be arriving soon. He was about to land at Aden Abdulle Airport, which was in the last southern district of Mogadishu, a city plagued by violent crime, terrorism, and civil unrest. A city that was constantly bombed by terrorist groups, like Al Shabab, but not just Al Shabab. Somalia was a breeding ground for new terrorist groups wanting a piece of the action, or just wanting more than what they had. They knew no better, death and destruction was all they knew, and it was the only way they knew how to get the government to listen. The government had no control in a country where seven out of ten lived in poverty.

But despite all the killings and despite all the bombings, Somalia was still a magnet for adventurous tourists. Somalia had the longest coastline out of all the African Countries, and this meant they had some of the best beaches in the world. Hundreds, if not thousands of western tourists would arrive each year, despite the dangers, just to relax and to swim off the beaches.

Please fasten your seatbelts, and fold away your food tray, and foot rests please. Welcome to Mogadishu.

This was Chris's first trip to Mogadishu and Somalia, but he'd done his research. He was under no illusions, and was well aware he was about to land in one of the most dangerous countries, and cities in the world. It had baffled him, learning just how many tourists it attracted. Not just westerners, but people from all around the world, however, it was the westerners that were more vulnerable, to attack.

Chris weaved his hands through his long blond hair while eyeing up a young hostess that he had found to be quite beautiful. She was dressed in her traditional dress, which was just a single length of fabric, in this case red silk, which they cleverly weave around their bodies to make a dress; she also wore a hijab which just enhanced her beautiful face. But that was as far as it went with Chris; unlike his good friend John, he was happily married. Also, despite her obvious young age, he was sure she'd be married. It was common for girls to get married at ages younger than fifteen, but not always for love, but because their parents had insisted on it. It was mainly because they could sell their child for more money than they could make in several years, but also because it was the best chance of them being able to give their child a better life.

Chris had taken some relief in knowing he won't actually have to go into the centre of Mogadishu. The resort he was to visit was in Jazeera, about eight miles south of the city, apparently there were several resorts and hotels in the same area, and also it was an area protected by the government. It was an area cordoned off right down to the beach, and it was an attempt by the government to increase tourism by making them feel secure. That obviously hadn't worked, and it was Chris's suspicion that that was the whole idea. Who ever had committed this terrible crime, it was

The Journalists - Congo Rescue

Chris's suspicion their intention was to punish the government, probably for not listening to their pleas. They would have known that the government had spent millions and by killing tourists, it would have cost the government in revenue.

The plane landed on the tarmac with relative ease, before making its way to the arrivals gate. Chris was eventually making his way to luggage claim, while looking around the relatively new airport. There weren't much to see, one airport was the same as the other as far as he was concerned, all selling duty-free goods and expensive souvenirs that just weren't worth the money.

Chris was feeling some anxiety, not much, just a little, after he'd collected his rucksack and was about to enter into the arrivals lounge. It wasn't anything new and he knew John was the same. It was when people arriving in dangerous countries were at their most vulnerable, especially if they'd never arrived at that country before. They'd have no idea which way the taxi driver was taking them. Young taxi drivers were the worst, for just a few Somali shillings they'd drive their passengers into some quiet districted and straight into the hands of terrorists.

As Chris exited the airport a stream of perspiration that had built up in the terminal, ran down his face finding its way down to his chin, where it dripped off. It wasn't because of the anxiety or because he was faced with dozens of young taxi drivers, but it was just that bloody hot.

He searched around looking for someone he thought might be most suitable to take him to his location, while being stampeded by the young taxi drivers, all trying to catch his fare. It didn't help with them knowing that westerners were usually quite generous at tipping, and Chris knew he was no exception. Looking over the heads of what must have been two dozen begging youngsters, he spotted an old fella leaning on his taxi. He would have loved to have been able to help one of the youngsters, who he was sure needed the money, but the risk far outweighed what he actually wanted to do. He weaved his way through the young boys, to finally approach the old fella. 'Jazeera Complex,' John said, while the old fella smiled at him with a look partly of shock, and partly of surprise. Chris was sure he got very few fairs here, and that was because of the youngsters.

'Come we go,' he said. He stretched his arm out pointing to the passenger side. He himself was soon being harassed by the youngsters so he had to scramble into his taxi rather rapidly. After he was sitting comfortably behind the wheel he said. 'Okay, now we go.'

John was satisfied with his choice and felt sure he could relax during the short journey, which he knew was only about eight miles, and would lead them away from the city of Mogadishu.

'You, Americani?'

Chris turned to look at the old fella, whom was as black as black could be, and had more wrinkles than a badly made bed. His very short, white hair neatly knitted to his head.

'No, I'm British.'

'Ah, Britannia, I like Britannia,' he then went on to sing. 'Britannia, Britannia all the way,' then ending with a croaky like chuckle.

Chris sniggered slightly; he actually liked the old fella.

'You holiday?' the old fella asks, smiling at Chris, his smoke stained teeth glaring at him.

'No, I'm here to work.'

'Ah, you work,' the old fella paused. 'What work?'

'I'm a Journalist.'

'Ah, jourlist, today many jourlist.'

Chris had never heard it pronounced quite like that, but knew what he meant. Actually, he wasn't at all surprised, he knew there was going to be a press conference later this afternoon, he was sure journalists from all over the world be there. A western family was massacred, if there was ever an attention seeker this was it.

Chris at this point knew very little about the family that was murdered, other than they were western. German, he'd considered, American…he knew how unpopular the Americans were here. He'd seen the movie, he knew what happened. He'd seen the terrible recordings of the American Ranger being dragged through the streets. He was a soldier himself at the time which had made it all the more painful.

The area they were driving through wasn't bad at all. Nice villas, decent roads, and even palm trees that were planted in the centre dividing barrier. But they were still quite close to the airport and now quite close to their location. It was obvious enough if you wanted to attract tourists, the route from the airport would need to look at least half decent. He was also sure the people living in this area weren't your average citizens, probably business men, or government officials. Somalia was a place where the average civilians were treated like dogs, and regularly beaten by government soldiers to keep them in line, Chris sighed as he thought about it.

'Now to much soldier, big problem for me,' the old fella said.

Chris had already noticed the closer they got to their location the more soldiers there were. 'Why problem,' Chris asked.

'Can't take Somali passengers into Jazeera, no passengers, no money.'

'Um.' Chris could understand the old fella's woes, and the checkpoint a head just emphasized what he'd said.

They pulled up to the checkpoint slowly, but didn't even have to stop before they were waved on by the soldier manning it.

'No, problem,' Chris said.

'You not Somali.'

'Um, good point.'

'Jazeera Complex, yes?'

'Yes,' Chris said. The Jazeera Complex was not actually where the press meeting was going to be held, or was it where the other journalist would be staying, it was actually where the family was murdered. Chris had been to lots of press conferences and most of them were a useful means of getting to the truth, as well as making it easier and quicker to complete his report, but here, in this in this part of the world. Chris knew better. A western family was murdered while under their protection, or at least under their promised protection. They will say what they have to say to steer the blame away from them, and their so called security.

'Too much soldier,' the old fella said again.

Chris looked forward and saw there were at least three soldiers at the entrance. It was to be expected, but did lead him to wonder whether they were there during the murders. He'd also wondered if the resort would be closed, but that idea was soon dismissed after seeing an Arabic family leave and climb into a topless jeep, which was parked at the entrance.

'Jazeera Complex,' the old fella announces. 'You sure you stay here, Britannia?'

'Yes, I'm sure,' Chris said. He knew to the taxi driver it would seem strange and he could understand why he had asked. He was also sure that the rest of the reporters would be staying at the many hotels that dotted the area.

The old fella looked deep into Chris's eyes. 'You sure you jourlist?'

'Yes, of course,' Chris insisted.

He paid the old fella his fare, and a respectable amount more, before climbing out of the taxi only to hear the old fella say.

'I like Britannia very much.'

The Journalists - Congo Rescue

Approaching the resort's entrance, he couldn't help but notice the look on the soldiers faces. It was a look that said, here comes another crazy westerner. About to enter and after nodding a friendly gesture to the soldiers, one of them raised his hand. He was without doubt the elder of the three, and well, didn't look too friendly.

'You cannot go inside,' he said, with a smirk indicating he was actually enjoying stopping Chris.

'Yes, I can, I have a booking,' Chris said, reaching into his top pocket. 'See,' Chris handed him his internet booking that he'd printed out before leaving the UK.

The soldier hardly looked at it before saying. 'You have to change, stay at hotel, this better.'

Chris could sense he was just being awkward. And was also sure he'd be under orders to treat westerner's politely. It was always the case after a terrible crime like this. 'No, I stay here,' Chris said then handed him his press card.

'Of course, sir, sorry, welcome, sir,' the soldier said, passing Chris his booking and press card and lifting his arm in the direction of the entrance, though with a clear look of annoyance on his face.

The Journalists - Congo Rescue

Chris knew not only would he be under orders to be polite to westerner's, but to be especially friendly to Journalists.

After passing through the main entrance that was a rather large arch with two gates that were opened, Chris took a quick scan of the resort and instantly could see the problem with having a resort like this in a place like this. He also noticed that one of the small bungalows was condoned off using yellow striped tape, it was bungalow nine. Shaking his head, he opened the small glass door that led into the reception area.

Two friendly smiles greeted him as he entered, an elderly couple stood behind the counter and as he approached they said in concert. 'Good morning, sir.'

Actually, it was just passed noon, but that didn't matter. 'Good morning - Chris Jones, I made an online booking,' Chris said, while noticing a woman behind him dressed all in black, and cleaning some ornaments.

'Okay, let me see,' the elderly woman said, before tapping the keys on the computer with remarkable ease for a woman of her age. She and her husband surprisingly enough wore western clothes, though she did wear a hijab with her quite colourful, but conservative blouse. Her husband wore a black suit and white shirt, and a very friendly smile.

'Ah, yes, here it is, Chris Jones. May I see your passport, please?'

Chris passed her his passport, while being impressed by her knowledge of the English language. He watched as she made a copy of it and gave it to him back. He then watched as she searched through the keys that hung on the wall in a small glass fronted box.

Judging by the amount of keys that were left in the box Chris could see the resort was only about twenty-five percent full. 'Is number eight available, it's just that it's my lucky number,' he said, with a small shrug and a fake smile.

'Yes, number eight, here it is. Caaishu, could you escort this gentleman to his bungalow.'

The young woman dressed all in black, which by the way was the main dress code for young women in Somalia, took the key from the elderly woman without saying a word, before opening the door that Chris had entered. Chris followed, knowing she wasn't allowed to talk to westerners, or anyone she didn't know. It made it all the more surprising when she asked with her head bowed. 'Are you British?'

The Journalists - Congo Rescue

Chris waited until he'd entered and was just in the doorway, but out of sight, before he answered. He knew how much trouble she'd be in if she was seen talking to him. 'Yes, I'm British,' he whispered, while taking the key from her.

She just gave him a small nod, before disappearing again. John found it strange but had a feeling he'd be seeing her again.

Chris glanced around the large room, but it could have looked like the queen of England's bedroom, or one of the many shithole's he'd seen during his travels, he didn't care. That wasn't why he'd chosen to stay there. Just in the next bungalow an entire family was mutilated just for being in the wrong place at the wrong time. These people knew nothing about the family they'd slaughtered; they were just a means of getting back at their government, obstacles that benefitted the government but not them. Chris was well aware how tough life could be, he'd seen it all, but that was no reason to destroy people's lives, people who knew nothing of their struggle, and people whom if did, would probably try to help.

That said, the room was quite nice, but the reason he was staying there was to try find out all he could about what had happened, things he was sure would not come to light at the press meeting.

The Journalists - Congo Rescue

He had a little more than an hour before the meeting was to start so decided to go for a walk around the resort, see what he could learn. He stood just outside the door of his bungalow first, and as he scanned his eyes around, just like when he'd first entered the resort, he could see the problems. Who'd ever designed the resort must have been thinking of somewhere else, somewhere safe, somewhere peaceful, and somewhere where there weren't terrorists living in just about every building, small apartment, and room with a window in Mogadishu.

Firstly the wall that encircled the resort, and was only about five feet and a bit, couldn't keep out the old fella that brought him there in the taxi. The area it covered was immense, probably the size of two football pitches, and would take an army of security guards to monitor every possible entry point.

Chris started to walk, passing the cordoned of bungalow, where there was a small parking area, his had one too, they all had one. He shook his head in shock and amazement, after making his way to the back of the bungalow. He'd seen what he'd expected to see, but hoped he wouldn't see - nothing. All the terrorists had to do was leap over the wall, and enter the bungalow through the back door which was more than a little flimsy, it was obvious, it lay on the floor in pieces. But what had made it all that more horrendous, was that they wouldn't have even been seen.

Chris hurried back to the front of the bungalow, he didn't want to be seen snooping, but he had been seen, the young woman dressed all in black had seen his every move. She'd been cleaning one of the bungalows on the opposite side of the resort, after an Egyptian family had just left. She'd seen something in Chris; she felt he was someone she could trust.

Chris continued his walk, and he was impressed, it was a beautiful resort. But he couldn't help but wonder what could have possessed a person to build such a complex in a country like this. Chris thought it might be money orientated; corruption can be a worse killer than terrorism. Money is a powerful temptation and can corrupt even the nicest of people, but here, it wouldn't have taken much. Chris had seen it all over this part of the world, building contractors were ten to a penny, and were happy to pay to secure a contract. It didn't end there, having already secured the contract the contractor would save money where possible, in this case the pathetic wall that encircled the complex.

The Journalists - Congo Rescue

Press conferences were sometimes useful if you wanted to put an official under pressure, if you ask the right questions you can even bring out the perpetrator of such corruption. Chris now found himself looking forward to such a meeting.

--Chapter Eleven--

THE SAHAFI HOTEL was one of the more expensive, if not the most expensive hotels in the area. It has five-hundred luxury rooms, two swimming pools, two restaurants, a spa, and a large conference room. Being only around three hundred metres from the Jazeera Complex, Chris had made his way there on foot. As he reached the half-moon shaped driveway that took you to the main entrance, he could see all the other Journalists arriving. CNN, BBC, Al Jazeera, they were all there, most of which carried a camera around their neck and a briefcase in their hands. Chris just had a pen and notebook. Taken pictures of corrupt officials who enjoyed their moment of fame just wasn't the way Chris worked. He also felt a little underdressed in his black jeans, and black polo T-shirt.

There was also a strong security presence as you'd expect, at a meeting like this, but Chris wore his press card around his neck so the soldiers let him pass.

About to enter the hotel Chris was stopped in his tracks. Someone had called his name, and the voice seemed familiar. He turned around to see a medium sized man in a white shirt and blue tie, his camera, as like all the rest was hanging around his neck.

'Ah, Peter, that's right isn't it.'

'Yes, Chris, you remembered.

'I did, but I'm sorry, because I'm not quite sure why,' Chris rubs his chin trying to remember.

Peter Newman chuckled slightly. 'Well, I guess you can be forgiven for that old chap, it was around fifteen years ago. We served in the Para's together, though only briefly; I believe you left to join the SAS.

Chris clicked his fingers as the memories came flowing back. 'Peter Newman, I do remember you; you're the skinny kid who could run like the wind.'

'That's me, though I'm a little slower these days, and a little fatter I'm afraid,' he said, holding his stomach.

'So, what the hell are you doing here, pal?'

'Same as you, old chap, I'm with the BBC. I *heard* you were a journalist now.' Peter scratched his head. 'Ah, that's right, John Stone told me, I believe you two are still good friends.'

'Yeah, I think we always will be, he works for the same agency as me. Actually, I've been meaning to give him a call; he's in the Congo.'

'Wow, so you guys are getting to visit all the nice places, then,' Peter said, smiling.

'Yeah, you too it seems.'

'Well, actually, up until now it hasn't been too bad, though this place does suck somewhat, daren't even leave the hotel. That poor family, they were from my part of the world you know.'

'Sorry?'

'Yeah, Bristol, Mother, Father, daughter, and son, I'd even met him once, lovely chap.'

Chris was left speechless, he hadn't even contemplated that they might come from the UK, and Peter mentioning there was a son and daughter was making his blood boil.

'You okay mate, you look a little distant. I'm guessing you didn't know they were from the UK.'

'Ah, no, no I didn't.' Chris said, shaking himself out of the initial shock.

'That's okay, old chap, I was the same when I first heard - shocking business.' Peter said, shaking his head. 'So, where you staying? I'm at the dolphin, quite a nice hotel actually, not that I'm not looking forward to leaving first thing in the morning, of course.'

'Jazeera Complex.'

'Say what, old chap!' Peter asks eyes wide open, and looking a little shocked.

Suddenly, a convoy of black Mercedes Benz's pulled up.

'Oh well, here we go, the officials have arrived,' Peter said, forgetting what they were just talking about.

The driver of the first car opened his door and climbed out of the vehicle. He then made his way to the passenger side rear door and opened it.

'Ah, that's Abshir Mohamed, chief of foreign affairs,' Peter said, as the quite tall, smooth shaven, quite good looking man exited his vehicle.

If appearances were anything to go by Chris felt he looked like a decent guy. But appearances weren't anything to go by, and he could have just as easily been an African Warlord.

The driver of the same car, then closed the door, and made his way to the other side, opening the rear door on the driver's side.

'Um, that's the Chief General,' Peter said. 'He's in charge of all these soldiers, and all security,' Peter added, as an overweight, man, with a white beard, and large bags under his eyes exited the vehicle with an intimidating look about him.

Chris growled under his breath.

Soon after, the rest of the drivers started to exit their vehicles.

'Come on, we'd better go inside,' Peter said, almost walking into the general, and receiving a not so friendly stare.

'Excuse me, Peter said, smiling and feeling slightly embarrassed.

Chris had taken an instant dislike to the general; he'd noticed the way he'd looked at Peter. He'd seen men like him before. They have a look about them, as if they thought they were better than everyone else, and felt it was their place to put other people in their place. They were cruel, heartless people, who felt it was their right to kill and maim, Chris could see this guy was just like that. He was now looking forward more than ever, for the meeting to start.

Chris couldn't help but notice the large, quite high stage at the front of the conference room. Six rows of chairs lined up in front of it, looking so small up against the large wooden structure. The hall was now starting to fill with Journalists, as the sound of the chairs scraping on the floor echoed around the hall. All the chairs were allocated to specific media companies so Chris wasn't able to sit near Peter, whom he was glad he'd met. He'd had a good knowledge of the people that had attended the meeting, and now Chris could be better prepared.

'So, maybe we can catch up after the meeting, hey old chap.'

'Yeah, that sounds good. I'll catch you later, then.'

Suddenly, the stage started to fill. There were three chairs either side of the stage where quite large men in black suits sat. Chris was sure they were there for security purposes. Abshir Mohamed, chief of foreign affairs and his general Bashir Hassan, sat at the centre of the stage behind a desk, and on the desks were their microphones. Abshir Mohamed wore a black suit not unlike his security. The general was in full military attire, his medals dangling from both sides of his jacket. Medals Chris doubted he deserved.

The room went quiet. 'Good morning, gentlemen.' Abshir Mohamed started. 'It is with sincere regret that this meeting has had to be held. It saddens me deeply the events that have taken place in my country. To think that a crime of this magnitude could have happened under our watch breaks my heart. I had made promises to keep all tourists safe from harm, and I have failed in that effort. My condolences go out to the relatives and families who knew the Hamilton family, which I have been informed, were very nice people. They arrived here in Mogadishu only two days previous to enjoy our wonderful beaches and to swim in the beautiful blue seas that we have, only to be slaughtered in their beds, while they slept.'

Chris was actually a little surprised, Abshir Mohamed was either a really good actor, or he did genially care. However, the look on the general's face told a completely different story.

'Okay, is there any questions, Abshir Mohamed asks, while looking at a list on his desk giving all the questions that were going to be asked and the media company that was going to be asking them.

The Journalists - Congo Rescue

The journalist's hands went up as though rehearsed.

'Yes, you, the man with the cream jacket.'

'Timothy Watson, CNN. It's said that there were no witnesses to the crime in mention, so is it realistic to think you can apprehend the men responsible for this terrible crime?'

Abshir Mohamed cleared his throat with a small cough. 'Yes, every effort is being taken, and all resources are being used to find and arrest the culprits of this vicious attack.' Abshir Mohamed cleared his throat again. 'Please, let me try to help you understand what this means. Mogadishu is a large city covering an area about the size of London, however, unlike London that might have a row of large houses with a family occupying each house. Mogadishu would have a family occupying each room. It's a city where all the occupants are frustrated and angry because of the way they have to live.'

If a mouse was to scamper across the room at this moment it would have been heard by everyone in the room.

'Because of this, dozens if not hundreds of small terrorist groups are formed with the same intention - destroy the government. We believe this was the case in this event, by targeting tourists, they knew it would harm the government by reducing desperately needed revenue. Now to answer your question….we are doing everything we can do, but the task is massive, and it will take time.

Chris was surprisingly impressed; this Abshir Mohamed wasn't like so many other government officials that he'd met. He wasn't lying, he wasn't making up excuses, but he was just telling it as it was, and in a way that made it very clear.

'Next question, please, Abshir Mohamed asks.'

The hands go up again.

'You, with the white shirt, and blue tie.'

'Peter Newman, BBC. With all the security present, and there's plenty I've seen them,' Peter said, while nodding his head.

The other Journalists chuckle, though quietly. Chris remains silent. Abshir Mohamed, smiles.

'Why was it possible for the terrorists to sneak passed your men, commit this horrible crime, then sneak out without even being seen or heard.'

Fair question, Chris thought, and was now looking forward to the answer.

'Um, that is a good question,' Abshir Mohamed said, with a look so serious. 'Let me try to explain, and I hope you don't mind if I use London again as an example. Scotland Yard and a police force that doesn't even need to carry weapons, unless there is a terrorist attack, or a crime of this nature. It's a Police force to be proud of and a police force where there is no corruption. The reason being, there's no need for corruption. All well paid, and all having a pension to look forward to when they retire, why would they jeopardize that? Here there is no police force, just the Somali army who has to fight to protect the Somali people from bordering countries, such as Ethiopia and Kenya, as well as try to police its own country. Their salary barely enough to feed their family and if god forbid, their hurt doing their job they will receive nothing from a government that has nothing. There's no retirement plan here, so if they're asked to turn a blind eye for an amount of money equaling their yearly salary, well, what are they to do. This doesn't even come close to excusing what happened. I'd promised you that I would protect the tourists and that was always my intention, but you can see what I'm up against.'

Abshir Mohamed even looked a little emotional, and Chris was sure he was genuine, something he hadn't seen in this part of the world for many years, if ever.

'Okay, next question, please, you…'

The Journalists - Congo Rescue

'Abshir Mohamed a man in politics and a man with feelings, this is a very rare thing in this part of the world.'

'Who is this man, he's not on the list,' Abshir Mohamed insists.

'I'll have him removed,' the general insists.

'A man I know I could grow to like,' Chris added with a warm smile aimed at Abshir Mohamed.

'No, let him speak.'

'But, Abshir.' The general was clearly furious.

'A man who is not afraid to tell it as it is, and a man who I believe is genially saddened by the recent events. So, I'm confused….why would a man like you, sir, allow the construction of a resort like the Jazeera Complex to be built in a city like Mogadishu, the same resort in which the Hamilton family resided.'

'That's it; I'll throw him out myself.'

'No, you'll sit there and be quiet, general.'

Abshir Mohamed turned to look at Chris, a man he'd just met, but someone he also felt he could like. 'Please sir, what is your name?'

'Chris Jones, sir, I work out of London for an independent agency, and yes the British police force is a force to be proud of.'

Abshir Mohamed smiles. 'So Chris, please elaborate, what is wrong with the Jazeera Complex.'

'Sir, you must allow me to remove this man.'

'General if you don't shut up, you'll be the one that is removed.'

'Please continue Chris.'

Chris looked at the general, who he could see he was furious, he allowed a small grin to appear on his face that was aimed at the man sat next to Abshir Mohamed. 'Sir, the Jazeera Complex is a security nightmare. It covers an area equal to the size of two football pitches. The wall that encircles the complex, and is meant to keep out terrorist groups like the ones you described so accurately, is only five feet tall. Any child could climb it. There are some thirty bungalows that all come with a door at the back, it's a door that any child could kick down, and it is a door that is out of sight, and it's only about five feet from the wall. The group that committed this crime had an easy job, sir, and it was due to the poor design of the Jazeera Complex.'

Abshir Mohamed remained silent for a moment. The general could hardly console himself; his fists clenched tight, his eyes protruding like some kind of alien.

The Journalists - Congo Rescue

Abshir Mohamed hadn't taken his eyes of Chris, and for some reason, at this moment, wished he was in charge of security. 'Are you sure you're, just a Journalist, Chris?'

'Yes, sir, absolutely.'

'So, Chris, if I may ask, why is it you know so much about the Jazeera Complex?'

'It's where I'm residing now, sir.'

There were gasps, and small chuckles throughout the room.

Interesting. 'Well, to answer this question, I'll hand it over to the man responsible for overlooking all blue prints to insure that all structures, mainly hotels, and resorts are safe for tourists and visitors alike, Mr. Bashir Hassan, our Chief General.'

If steam could come out of a man's ears, Chris was sure it would be coming out of the general's ears right now. He was tongue tied and confused, and obviously had never been treated in such a way. Suddenly he stood up in such a rage, his fists thumping down hard on the desk in front of him. He turned to look at Abshir Mohamed and speaking Somali he said.

'This is a disgrace, why would you embarrass me like this? I've been chief general for twenty years, why would you do this?'

The Journalists - Congo Rescue

'Why would you, Bashir, you know how important this is to me, and you know how important this is to the Somali people. You're the disgrace here, you have everything and it's still not enough, your people have nothing and you're still taking from them. It's people like you that stops progress in its tracks, don't you see that.'

The Journalists just sat there watching the two of them yell at each other in their local tongue, not one of them understanding, but all of them knew what it was about.

'Well, what do you think you, can do about it, you fool, you can't fire me, you don't have the authority,' Bashir Hassan said.

'No, you're right Bashir, but our president does.'

'So, you are going to speak to the president about me, just because of a few stupid westerners getting killed.'

Abshir stood up, he wanted to punch Bashir Hassan so much, but knew that would only look bad on him, and weaken his case against him. 'Get out of here before I have you thrown out in front of all these Journalists.'

Bashir Hassan looked at the Journalist's knowing that that would be one embarrassment too far. He straightened his collar, while trying to look like nothing had happened, he then left the room.

Abshir Mohamed sat down again; he took a couple of deep breaths while trying to compose himself. 'I'm sorry about that, gentleman, politics, hey. Well, I guess that's the end of the meeting, thank you all for coming, and have a safe flight home.'

Chris and Abshir exchanged grins, and even a small wink.

The journalists picked themselves up off their chairs and grabbed their briefcases before starting to leave. Chris also made his way to the entrance while being followed closely by Peter Newman.

'Wow, you don't hold your punches, hey, old chap,' Peter said, once they were outside.

'It had to be said. I've seen people like that Bashir Hassan all my life, it's people like that that keeps people down, he isn't fit to be a general.'

'Well, you told him, right, but John, now I'd keep a low profile, go back to your room and stay there until tomorrow, that general was pissed, and who knows what kind of friends he has.'

'But what about our drink, pal?'

'Huh, I'm sorry old chap, but I'm going to keep my distance from you, nothing personal old chap, but I'm out of here.' Peter said, now walking in the direction of his hotel.

'Okay, pal, have a good flight,' Chris said, watching Peter head off down the road. He wasn't bothered about Peter; he knew it had to be said. Chris weaved his hands through his long blond hair, with a satisfying feeling flowing through his veins. He started to leave too, although feeling a little guilty, not because of the general, but because of Abshir Mohamed.

--*Chapter Twelve*--

A GUIITY FEELING pumped around Chris's body along with a feeling that the job was not yet finished. The Hamilton family lye dead in the city morgue and no one had been apprehended for the crime. That didn't sit well with Chris and he knew it wouldn't have sat well with his good friend John. He sat there for a while wondering what his pal would do, even though deep down he knew. He remembered what Abshir was saying about how many terrorist groups could be living in Mogadishu, and making it clear that finding the group that committed the crime was going to take time. He didn't have time, if it was going to happen at all, it was going to have to happen tonight. He knew marching into Mogadishu looking for a needle in a haystack in a place where every family in every room had a gun, was not the way to go. He knew there was only one option, and that was to bring them to him.

He'd remembered the woman dressed all in black, she'd asked if he was British, why would she ask that, he wondered, she had to know something he was sure of it. Chris now lye on his bed, his head on the pillow, and his hands weaved together behind his head, it was clear she was his only chance, and knew all he could do for now, was wait, and hope she comes.

Chris had fallen asleep, waking up some time later in the same position, with the back of his head on the pillow. Lifting his arm, he glanced at his watch, it was 6.00 o'clock in the evening. Sitting up and swinging around on his backside, he got off the bed to make a cup of tea, or coffee. He'd noticed the kettle in the small kitchen area and hoped there'd be some coffee or tea there. He smiled when he saw there were three tea bags and three sachets of coffee. He'd had to make some very difficult decisions throughout his career, but didn't think choosing coffee or tea could be so bloody difficult.

After finally choosing the coffee, he glanced over to the small, window which had been letting the light in, but now was just dark. He closed the small curtain hurriedly, knowing with his light on he could easily be seen from outside, he didn't want to make an easy target for some lone terrorist. He was sipping on his coffee when he heard what he'd been waiting for, a quiet tap on the door, a tap that could only have been a woman.

He opened the door and grabbed her arm, pulling her inside while looking around outside to make sure no one had seen, he knew her life would depend on it. She was clearly very scared, and her hands were shaken uncontrollably. Her sweet, young face looked terrified, and Chris guessed her age around eighteen. He wanted to hold her, to reassure her, but she was Muslim and he knew she'd probably never been held before, at least not by a westerner, and definitely not by someone she didn't even know. He thought that might be more frightening than the reason she'd come here. He was a little surprised, now he could see she was younger than he thought.

'Calm down. It's okay, no-one knows you're here.' Chris said, wanting to hold her hand, but not quite sure he should. 'Do you mind if I ask your name?'

It's Caaishu. I'm sorry, but I had to come. I loved them, they were so nice. I played with their children. They were so sweet and so well behaved.' She raised her head from the bowing position to look at Chris. 'They didn't deserve this; they didn't deserve to die like this.' Tears poured from her eyes and run down her dark cheeks. 'I know who did it!' she said, her face now full of hatred.

Chris fetched her a small hand-towel that had been hanging in the bathroom. As she wiped the tears from her face, it was clear how upset she was, but he'd seen people in this state many times, and he could see she was just as angry as she was sad.

'Please, sit here on the bed,' Chris said, reaching a hand out and speaking in his softest tone. He pulled out a chair from under a small table and positioned it directly in front of her; he could see she needed to calm down a little first, so he waited. Eventually she'd calmed down and looked at Chris, but still with tears running down her cheeks. 'His name is Abdirahim Ali, and he's a vicious monster,' she started, shaken again at the mention of his name.

'It's okay, you're safe here, tell me more about this Abdirahim Ali.'

The Journalists - Congo Rescue

'He lives in the Bagmada Kaaraan district, an area at the centre of Mogadishu. It's quite close to the coast. It's, what was it you westerners like to say? A real shithole.' She was finally calm enough to release a small chuckle.

Chris had to laugh too, hearing that coming from a young Muslim girl was hilarious. But it didn't last; she soon wore her more serious face as she continued to speak.

'But it's my home and my family's home too, I've always lived there, but it's hell, at least it is now.'

Chris could see she liked talking to him, it was for sure she didn't mind westerners, he'd heard what she'd said about the Hamilton family. 'What did you mean, it is now?'

'Now, because, Abdirahim Ali is living there. He moved into the district about two years ago, for the young men in the district he was something new, something fresh, someone that gave them hope. He'd give speeches, promising to take down the government and give the city back to the people, he even talked about taking Somalia back, it was nonsense of course, but for the young men it gave them hope of something better, those poor men had nothing, no hope and no future.'

The Journalists - Congo Rescue

Chris could see why terrorist groups were springing up everywhere, it gave them meaning, and it gave them a sense of purpose. Having nothing made you vulnerable to people like this Abdirahim Ali, especially young men.

'He killed the head official in our district, a corrupt man who had everything while the people barely had enough to eat. After this his popularity grew strong. The young men in the district followed him like he was a god or something.'

Chris understood completely.

'He and the young men would steal from anyone who had something, and they would give it to the people who had nothing. He was loved by everyone, even the elderly warmed to him. But then everything started to change.'

'What do you mean, what started to change?' Chris asked, but had an inkling of what she was going to say.

'He'd killed anyone who was anyone in the district, and had robbed anyone who had anything, which of course just left the poor, the same people he'd helped. Now they're his victims. Now the district lives in fear, and no one dares to go up against him.'

Her story was a familiar one to Chris, he knew how power can take over a man, and he knew what a man would do just to hold on to it. It was beginning to make sense to him, but he had to ask one last question. 'So, why kill the Hamilton family, they meant nothing to him, and this area is miles away from your district.'

'It was because of what our president had said. He'd promised to improve the lives of everyone in Mogadishu first, before improving the lives of Somali people in general, and the money was going to come from tourism. He'd promised to build new schools, new homes, and promised there'd be better security.'

Everything suddenly seemed so clear. This Abdirahim Ali knew if things were to improve, and there were signs of hope, not only would he loose his hold over the district, he'd be the first to be taken out. He'd killed the Hamilton's just to stop that from happening.

'I'm sorry…'

'Chris, my name is, Chris.'

'Chris, I'm sorry, I don't mean to burden you with all this, it's just that I saw you looking around the bungalow next door, I thought you might be able to help, but now I see that's not possible, you're just a journalist, what could you possibly do.'

'If you really thought that why would you have risked your life just to see me?'

'I don't know, I guess I was just hoping for the impossible, and you'd told me you were British, I'm guessing you're just as angry as me.'

'Huh, angry, it's way passed that now. This Abdirahim Ali has murdered this whole family that he didn't even know, just so he can continue to rule his district, and make your life and the lives of the people living there miserable.' Chris said, with visions of the two children being murdered by the animal.

'But what can *we* do?' Caaishu asks, with a look of hopelessness.

'We can kill him, Caaishu, that's what we can do.'

'But…'

'What can you tell me about his men, and how many of them are seen as his main men?' Chris knew for him to rule an entire district, he would need men close to him, men that he could rely on and help keep the rest of the men in line.

The young woman was trying not to stare, she'd never met anyone like Chris, especially someone who had long, blond her. She'd seen photos of western women with long blond hair, and the mother of the Hamilton family had long fair coloured hair. But he was a man, a strong man, of this she was sure, just looking at his muscles had awaken emotions that she never even knew she had. She'd stare at his long, blond hair and the way it laid on his shoulders, enhancing his tanned face and his blue eyes. He was without doubt the most handsome man she'd seen, if not a little strange too.

'Well, there's Cabdi Ahmed, he and Abdirahim are always together, I guess you could call him his number two. If Abdirahim wants anything done, he usually tells Cabdi first and he instructs Absame and Abshir Hassan to inform the men, their brothers by the way, and not nice people.

'So, do you know who exactly it was - that killed the Hamilton family, I mean?'

'Yes, it was the four of them, I heard them talking about it, or rather laughing about it. They were acting like only the four of them could have done it, like no one else could have pulled it off.' Caaishu started to cry again. 'Those bastards were even laughing about cutting the young boys head off.'

Chris could feel himself becoming angry, very angry.

The young woman had become upset again, it was thinking about the young boy who she'd played with that had done it. Chris could tell she'd spent quite a bit of time with westerners, just hearing her use words that were not in your average language course made it clear.

'Okay, I need you to listen to me, but you can't tell a soul what I'm about to say….I'm not just a Journalist I have also spent time in the military, and have dealt with people like this Abdirahim Ali before. The problem is, me being western there's no way I can go into Mogadishu because I'd standout like a Muslim would if he was to go to my local church.' Chris said, grinning.

Caaishu wanted to laugh but felt this was no time for laughing, especially now that Chris has admitted who he really was. She'd felt there was something about him, and now she was learning what that something was, and with enthusiasm flowing though her veins.

'So, what we need to do, Caaishu, is bring them to me, to bring them here.'

Chris was slightly surprised when he saw the look on her face, it was a look of enthusiasm, and not what he was expecting. But that soon changed, when the look became confused, and concerned.

'But won't that be dangerous, for you, I mean.'

Chris put a hand on each of Caaishu's shoulders. 'Don't worry about me, I know how to take care of myself, but I'm going to need your help, Caaishu, and I'm going to need your trust.'

'Okay, Chris, what do you need me to do?'

'Okay, then. First, I need you to give me a full description of these four men, starting with Abdirahim Ali.

--Chapter Thirteen--

ONCE UPON A time, people took pride in the upkeep of their property, as well as their community. They'd paint the exterior walls, even though they knew they'd probably be full of bullet holes by morning. They'd stain the shutters even though they were sure they'd be blown off the wall if there was a car bombing. They'd even clear the streets of brick rubble, after a rival Jihadist group had entered their district with RPG's. But not now, now they just didn't care.

The Journalists - Congo Rescue

As Caaishu walked through her streets after being dropped off by her employers, it was impossible to not see the bullet holes in the walls, and the shutters hanging on one hinge. She also had to watch her step as she navigated her way through the brick rubble that was all over the streets and had been there for as long as she could remember. But on this night she had hope that someday things would go back to how it was. It was never Palm-Springs and bared no resemblance to Disneyland. But the people were happy, and they'd make that extra effort to make the district at least habitable. People would sing as they walked down the streets. Children would play on the patches of waste land and in the charred buildings that lay empty. The small cafes would be full of people eating their local delicacy. Shops were opened till the early hours selling anything from garments, to Guntino's which the women wrapped around themselves to make a dress.

As Caaishu made her way home she, didn't even blink at the sound of sporadic gunfire coming from the next street, no one did. It was something the community had become used to. Gunfire and small explosions had replaced the sounds of people singing and children playing. The entrance door to Caaishu's building lay on the floor covered in brick rubble, while rats scampered from underneath the rotten object. After reaching the door to her room which was on the third floor, she knocked twice, and then three times, before finally knocking just the once. It was their way of knowing who was at the door. Caaishu smiled after her mother had opened the door with a smile that was just as blatant. They hugged before entering and once inside the door was locked using three large bolts.

'Hello father,' Caaishu said, before also giving *him* a hug.

He was sitting on the old couch that sat him about a foot off the floor. It was easier for him, having only one leg after having it blown off by an RPG. The rest of the family used large cushions which was the more traditional method.

'Caaishu,' her mother called. She'd prepared the evening meal and after giving her husband his dish on the sofa, she sat on the floor waiting for her daughter to join her. She'd made Sambusa, a fried pastry dish filled with either a spicy minced meat or vegetables, tonight it was vegetables. 'How was your day my dear?'

'Good mother, it was a good day.'

There wasn't a day that went by without her mother asking if she'd had a good day, and not once did Caaishu say she didn't. Her mother was so proud of her daughter; she'd only just turned eighteen and was already the main bread winner. But she never complained, she loved her parents and would do anything if it made them just that little bit happier. Her mother had noticed something about her daughter this evening, but didn't like to ask, she knew she'd tell her when she was ready. There was a spark in her eyes, a shine on her face, a look that had made her appearance that little more cheerful.

She had hoped she'd be married by now, but it just hadn't happened, she'd had plenty of offers, not Caaishu, but she. Men of all ages and stature had offered her money, most of which were too old for her, let alone her daughter, and some had offered more money than she'd ever seen. But she would never sell her Caaishu, not for all the money in the world. She knew Caaishu would marry anyone if that made them happy, but she wanted Caaishu to be happy, and she knew she could never be happy unless she married for love.

By 9.00 o'clock everyone was sleeping, at least Caaishu's parents were, despite the sound of gunfire just outside. Caaishu knew where the gunfire was coming from and who was causing the racket. She rose from her cushion to peep out the small window that looked out onto the main street.

The Journalists - Congo Rescue

There she could see Abdirahim's men shooting in the air as though they'd just won a battle, or had planted a bomb in a rival district. It was like this most evenings after they'd consumed more than enough alcohol, which was illegal here, Muslims don't drink alcohol, but these were not good Muslims. She searched her eyes up and down the street while looking for a person she hated with her very soul.

She'd noticed a group of men sitting outside a small café and it included the two brothers, Abshir and Absame Hassan, and as she looked on they were joined by two women dressed all in black. Caaishu was sure they were the girlfriends whom she knew, if only vaguely. She wondered if this might be her opportunity.

Being as quiet as she could not to wake her parents, she snuck out the door after she'd gotten dressed in the same clothes she'd been wearing that day, and the same clothes she'd seen the women wearing. She made her way towards where she'd seen the group while being stared, whistled, and yelled at by men she never knew or would ever want to know. It was scary, and she was scared knowing she'd never left the safety of her room at any time passed eight o'clock. It was now nine-thirty, but what had made it even scarier was the fact she was about to join the rowdy group she'd been watching.

As she passed them she turned to face them while at the same time trying to stay calm, she was sure someone would recognise her, especially one of the women.

'Caaishu is that you?' one of the women asked. It was Barwaaqo, a young woman in her mid twenties and who enjoyed hanging out with the men. She was just the person she'd hoped would be there. 'What are you doing out at this time?'

'I couldn't sleep, that's all, thought a walk might help,' Caaishu said in her most common voice.

'Come sit with us.'

'Nah, I'm okay, I think I'll head back home, but thanks anyway.'

'Come on, just for a while, I'll look after you.'

'Well, just for a moment, then.' Caaishu shook with fear, but knew she had to go through with it, she wanted her community back, and she wanted revenge for the Hamilton family.

'This is Caaishu, isn't she sweet,' Barwaaqo said, while introducing her to the group.

The brothers stared at Caaishu, and in a way that made her feel very uncomfortable. They wore scruffy checkered shirts though different colours over their thick set chests and broad shoulders, their faces, well, they were mean looking, and they for sure were not good looking. Both had shaven heads and short stubble beards. Caaishu's plan was working well, but she was terrified. She'd never mixed with people like this and as her hands shook under her clothing she hoped she never would have to again.

Absame Hassan passed Barwaaqo a glass and she picked it up and downed the alcohol in one.

'Whoa, that shit is strong,' she said, while smiling at her own achievement. 'Who made that stuff - it's as strong as hell.'

Absame smiled, and then winked. He then poured another. 'Let your young friend try it.'

'No, no, she's too young….'

'That's okay, just a little, it won't hurt.'

'I said no, Absame, she's too young.'

'That's okay, I'll try a little,' Caaishu said,' not wanting to, but wanting to hang out with them a little longer. She was waiting for an opportunity and waiting for them to start a particular conversation, in which they hadn't thus far. She took a small sip of the alcohol and it made her cough and splat all over the table as it burned on its way down. She'd never tasted anything so disgusting in all her life, and wondered how anyone would want to drink such awful stuff.

They all laughed at her, even Barwaaqo couldn't resist a small giggle. It didn't matter; they could laugh all they wanted, as long as they didn't tell her to go, not yet.

Suddenly, the two brothers stood up smiling. 'Where have you two been, out killing more western tourists?'

It had started. But it was obvious who the two brothers were talking to. Caaishu's legs started shaking, resting her hands on her knees, she tried to stop them. Her heart was beating hard and fast as Abdirahim Ali and Cabdi Ahmed joined them.

Abdirahim looked surprised to see an additional face with the group, a very young and beautiful face. Before sitting down, he rested his AK-47 up against the front wall to the small café. And Cabdi did the same. Abdirahim was tall; he wore camouflage trousers, a black vest, a black headscarf, and a string of ammo over his right shoulder. Cabdi was dressed the same though, he was a short, and a thickset man. Abdirahim was muscularly and had strong facial features and one eye slightly bigger than the other due to a piece of shrapnel nearly piercing his eye and leaving a scar right in the corner of his eye. His black skin dripped with sweat as he sat down opposite Caaishu. He was a daunting sight for anyone, but for Caaishu he was as scary as hell.

Abdirahim remained staring at the new face for some time before turning away and asking. 'So, where's my drink.'

'Yes, of course, sorry, Ali,' Absame said, Ali was what they called him, it was easier.

Absame poured his drink in the same glass that Caaishu had drank from. 'Here you are, Ali.'

The glass was full to the brim and Abdirahim downed it in one, while staring at Caaishu again. 'So, who is this?'

'This is Caaishu, she's no one, I asked her to sit here that's all,' Barwaaqo said, a little concerned for her young friend. She hadn't expected Abdirahim to turn up this early.

'So, Ali, I hear there was a press conference earlier, I bet Abshir Mohamed had a struggle on his hands trying to explain this one,' Absame said, laughing.

'Huh, I bet he did, not to mention that fat ass General of his, I just wish I could have been there,' Cabdi said.

'Well, as long as it keeps the tourists away, that's all that matters,' Abdirahim said, looking more than a little pleased with himself as he took another sip of the alcohol that he'd poured.

'Well, after what we'd done, I doubt they'll be any more westerners wanting to come and enjoy our beaches, they'd have to be crazy,' Abshir said.

They all laughed and picked up their glasses before clanging them at the centre of the table.

'But there are western tourists, I saw them checking in only this morning,' Caaishu mouth was dry from fear, and she only just managed to get the words out.

'Huh, I think that alcohol's gone straight to her head, silly girl,' Barwaaqo said, and now wishing she hadn't asked Caaishu to sit there.

'Checking in where,' Abdirahim was more than a little curious, he had his spy's and no one had said anything. He was sure she must have meant at one of the hotels that were far too secure.

Caaishu put her hand on her head. 'Maybe it was the alcohol speaking, I'm sorry.'

'Where,' Ali asked again, only a little louder.

'The Jazeera Complex, I work there, but…'

Abdirahim's eyes opened wide, a snarling grin appeared on his face. 'How many.'

'It was a family, I think, I don't know,' she said, still holding her head, and acting terrified, it wasn't hard, she was terrified.

The Journalists - Congo Rescue

Abdirahim thumped his hand down on the table; the small glasses hit the concrete below and smashed, Caaishu heart nearly jumped out of her chest.

'Why do I pay those soldiers when they don't tell me what I need to know?' Suddenly, he went quite, deep in thought, he was considering something. *Um, she work's at the Jazeera Complex, what could be better, a spy working just where I need her to be.* 'Come, on Cabdi we can handle this one.'

'But what about us, Ali?' Absame asked, while wanting to join them, he could still see the way the mother looked at him while he cut her throat.

'You two can stay here and take care of our new informant, give her whatever she needs and don't take your eyes off her for a moment.'

'Okay, Ali, we can do that,' Absame said, looking at Caaishu and wondering exactly what Abdirahim meant when he said give her whatever she needs. He knew what he needed as he continued to stare at her sweet young innocent face.

Caaishu knew she was in big trouble, she'd hoped at this point she could have gone home, but suddenly it didn't matter, as long as her new friend kills Abdirahim Ali, and his second in charge, Cabdi Ahmed, nothing else mattered.

Ali and Cabdi went to pick up their Toyota Corolla; it was a daft little car but attracted zero attention.

Abdirahim Ali wasn't overly eager to kill another western family, but his intentions were clear in his head. In his district, he was a god, no one dared mess with him, and if he wanted something it was his for the taking, whether that was drugs, alcohol, or a pretty young girl. People feared him, and he loved that, and no government was going to take that away, even if that meant another innocent family had to die.

--Chapter Fourteen--

THEY WERE ON the same route that Chris's taxi had taken and Abdirahim had told Cabdi to keep his eye on the ball, he knew there was a check point ahead and if they were to go too far they'd be seen.

'Turn right, here you fool.' Abdirahim shook his head.

'Oh, sorry Ali,' Cabdi knew he'd nearly missed the turn.

They were now on a route heading east and away from the coast, and the same route they'd taken the last time. They carried on for about a thousand metres before turning again down a small track that was rarely used, and run parallel to the original route. Ahead was another checkpoint, but this checkpoint had a young soldier manning it that they'd paid only the other night.

'What are you two doing here? I haven't contacted you. I haven't seen any westerners.'

Abdirahim exited the vehicle and approached the young soldier. 'Are you sure you haven't seen any westerners.'

The young soldier never wanted to help Abdirahim but he'd needed the money, and now he was wishing he hadn't. 'I'm telling you I haven't seen any, what…'

Before he could finish what he was saying, Abdirahim had forced his jagged edged knife into his gut, then pulled it out and slit his throat.

'Cabdi, give me a hand.'

They dragged the young soldier's body to where it couldn't be seen, before continuing down the small track. 'Who'd he think he was messing with, me, no one messes with me.'

'That's right,' Cabdi said.

But even Cabdi had thought that was unnecessary, and for the very first time doubted his leaders thinking. He was just a young man trying to support his family, and he was a Somali man to boot. If it was a westerner Cabdi knew he wouldn't have been thinking the way he was.

They could see the Jazeera Complex just ahead, approaching from the side no one could see them arriving. They parked up the vehicle. 'Leave the guns here, we won't need them,' he said, holding up the blood stained knife that he'd used to kill the young soldier.

They then snuck up to the wall. But just about to climb it and for no reason at all Abdirahim had a change of mind, and Cabdi could see something wasn't right about his leader.

'What is it Ali?' Cabdi whispered.

'I don't know. Something doesn't feel right.' He started to think about the young soldier he'd killed. He knew he'd paid him a lot of money to give them information, and he knew how much the young man needed it. 'The young soldier I killed, why would he not tell us if there were westerners staying here?'

'Well, don't you think you should have asked that before you slit his throat?'

He then started to think about the young girl who'd given him the information, he hadn't paid her, and there was no real reason why she should give him such information, she didn't even know him, and she worked here, why in hell would she risk losing all that, and for someone she didn't even know? 'Cabdi, I think I've messed up. Cabdi did you hear what I said.'

Cabdi gave Abdirahim a strange stare before dropping to the floor in a heap. Abdirahim stood there momentarily in a state of shock as he glanced upon a seven inch kitchen knife protruding out of Cabdi's back.

'That little bitch.' He reached in his pocket for his phone. *If I'm going to die that little bitch is going to die too.* He started to dial a number while searching his eyes into the darkness which he knew was just a patch of wasteland. About to dial the last number he heard a whistling sound coming out from the darkness, he saw something but then it was gone. He looked back around to finish the call, but he couldn't, the phone wasn't there, nor was his hand, just a large machete that he'd seen lying on the sand. He screamed out in pain while watching a tall figure appear from the darkness. 'Who the hell *are* you?'

Suddenly Abdirahim's worst fears became reality, he was about to die at the hands of a westerner, someone he'd seen as an infidel all his adult life and beyond. A man who didn't deserve to share the same air as him. Chris bent down and pulled the knife from his man's back.

'You can't kill me, infidel, you…'

Chris had thrust the knife into his throat and watched while the life in him left his eyes.

'Please, put the knife down, sir.'

Chris pulled the knife out of Abdirahim's throat while he watched his body slide down the wall. Chris wasn't so surprised to see a soldier there staring at him and the body of Abdirahim that was laying by his feet, he'd heard him scream too, he guessed the whole district probably heard. But he was surprised to see a soldier that looked quite like this one.

'Sir, who is that, and who is he?' The young, good looking soldier asked.

'This is Abdirahim Ali and this is Cabdi Ahmed, these are the bastards that killed the Hamilton family, now I have to go.'

'Go where sir?'

'The Bagmada Kaaraan district,' Chris said, somewhat surprised that the young soldier wasn't pointing his gun at him. He was confused. This young soldier who wore a black, beret like the one he used to wear in the Special Forces, and spoke with a slight accent, had just witnessed him kill two of his citizens, and all he could say was, 'go where sir'. 'You're not going to try and stop me?'

'How do you aim to get there, sir?'

Chris couldn't quite register what was going on. 'Why….in their vehicle, of course.'

'Okay then, I'm coming too,' he said while following Chris to the vehicle.

'Whoa, what the hell.'

'I'll explain on the way, sir.'

Chris scratched his head before getting into the vehicle and watching as the young soldier join him. He was still confused though at the same time grateful. It was obvious enough the young soldier wasn't there to arrest him, and where he was going he needed all the help he could get. The vehicle had an awful smell about it and Chris was sure he knew what it was.

'What, is that smell?' The young soldier asked.

'Death, there's been a few dead bodies in this vehicle.'

'How would you know that?' the young soldier asked while full of curiosity, especially after he'd seen the two terrorists that he'd killed.

'I'm a journalist we get to see it all.'

'Whoa, you're going to have to do better than that, I just saw you kill two Jihadists without even working up a sweat, or are Journalist trained in hand to hand combat these days.'

Chris looked at the young soldier who reminded him of himself when he was young and when he was in the Special Forces. He found himself not wanting to lie to a fellow soldier. 'I was in the British Special Forces.'

'Wow, I knew it had to be something like that.'

'You can't tell anyone, right,' Chris said, looking the young man straight in the eyes.

'No, sir, understood, sir.'

'So, what's your story anyway, why did you not apprehend me?'

'Apprehend you, no, I'm here to watch over you,' the young soldier now had to wonder why, after he'd seen what Chris was capable of.

'Watch over me, why, under whose orders?'

'Abshir Mohamed, sir.'

'Ah, the foreign affairs chap, I actually liked him, he seemed like a genuine guy.'

'He is, sir, and he liked you too,' the young soldier said, then shrugged. 'That's the reason I'm here.'

'How well do you know the Bagmada Kaaraan district,' Chris asked, he'd been so desperate to help Caaishu he hadn't even thought about it.

'Not a problem, I know it well.'

Chris smiled to himself now feeling very grateful, for meeting Abshir Mohamed. 'That general who was with Abshir Mohamed, there was something very off about that guy.'

'Huh, I wouldn't worry about him, sir, he's been put behind bars, and they won't be giving him the key anytime soon.'

'Really!'

'Yes, after the press conference, Abshir, had him investigated, they found out he'd been accepting bribes for years, and not just from building contractors.'

'Um, I can't say I'm too disappointed about that.' Chris was feeling pleased with himself knowing he'd played a big part in him being arrested, though even he was surprised it was so easy, it was just another reason to be grateful he'd met Abshir Mohamed. 'So, what's with the beret?'

'Special Forces, sir. Trained in Cairo. It's part of our president's plan to rain in on the Jihadists.'

Chris liked what he was hearing; he knew that having the right men in government made all the difference. 'Well, that is good to hear, because we're about to go kill some.'

The Journalists - Congo Rescue

Chris arrived at the small checkpoint; he'd taken the same route that he'd seen Abdirahim take.

'Something is wrong, there's no one manning the checkpoint,' the young soldier noted. He grabbed his gun and exited the vehicle to take a look. 'Sir, he's over here.'

Chris was in a hurry, but he was also curious, he knew this was the route that the jihadists took to enter Jazeera.

'He's dead, sir,' the young soldier said, looking at his comrade laying there in the dirt.

Chris bent down over the body.

'What are you doing?''

'I need a gun,' Chris said,' tucking the soldier's pistol down the back of his trousers.

'Do you think it was those two that you killed?'

'Without a doubt,' Chris agreed. He felt for the young man who stood looking at his comrade. 'Come on, there's more of them in the Bagmada Kaaraan district.'

Chris got back in the vehicle with some urgency, and was soon joined by his new friend. 'So, do you have a name?'

'Abu Hassan, sir, but you can call me Abu.'

'Abu, alright then.'

'Sir, how is it you know so much?'

'That's why we're going into Mogadishu, I have a young informant and she might be in danger.'

'She, sir?'

'Yeah, she's a young woman, one of the bravest I've seen. She works at the Jazeera Complex, she knew the Hamilton family. She came to my room and told me she knew who murdered them, I killed two of them back there, but she said there were four, I'm guessing she's now with the other two.

'So, how was it you managed to kill those two back at the Jazeera Complex, did you know they were coming? I mean they hadn't even entered it.'

'Yes, it was all part of the plan; I couldn't go into Mogadishu so we had to lure them to me, but I was hoping all four would come, now I'm worried for Caaishu.'

'Caaishu, that's a beautiful name, so I'm guessing she told them you were staying at the Jazeera Complex knowing they'd come after you.'

'Close, but not quite, she told them that there was another western family that had checked in, we had both decided that that would be more of a temptation.'

'Wow, and she did this all alone, she must be so brave.'

'Like I say, the bravest I have seen.'

*

Caaishu trembled as she sat watching Absame and his brother drink glass after glass of the awful alcohol that she'd tried and spat out. Her heart beating like a drum she prayed that she'd never have to see the face of Abdirahim Ali again, she hoped beyond measure, and prayed that Chris had killed him by now, because she knew if she was to lay eyes on him again, it would be her who would be killed.

But at this moment it was Absame and his brother that had her worried and the not knowing what they were going to do. She hadn't liked the way they had looked at her, and knew it was only because they were waiting for Abdirahim that they hadn't done anything, and the fact he'd told them to take care of her. She'd heard what drink can do to a man, and was now witnessing it first hand as the two brothers became more aggressive and more rowdy with each glass. Yelling and throwing things at passers-by, and acting like they owned the district.

'Okay, I'm going home, I have to work tomorrow,' Caaishu said, not thinking it was going to be that easy, but figured it was worth a try.

The Journalists - Congo Rescue

'Oh, you're going are you,' Absame said, now stood up and staggering around the small table that had stood between them and Caaishu. 'Sweet little Caaishu wants to go home,' he said, his face up close to hers his breath reeking of alcohol.

Barwaaqo stood up and approached the man she once liked to call her boyfriend, though now wondering why. 'Come on Absame, let the poor little thing go, we can go to my place, you'd rather have a real woman, right.' She no more wanted to sleep with him than Caaishu did, but she felt guilty, it was her who'd called her over after all. She put her hand on his shoulder. 'Absame you know what Abdirahim will do if you hurt her, let her go.'

Without warning Absame brought the back of his hand around catching Barwaaqo's face and sending her over the table where she landed on the floor in a heap.

Caaishu shook violently, as she saw what Absame had done to Barwaaqo, blood now dripping from her mouth, him with a face full of rage as he stared at her through lusting eyes.

'Abshir, let's take her upstairs and show her what real men can do.'

Caaishu tried to pull away, to release herself from Absame's grip, but he was too strong. 'Yeah, let's take her upstairs,' Abshir said, now grabbing Caaishu's other arm.

Caaishu had never felt so valuable; she had no defence against two strong men, she wanted to scream, but knew it was fruitless, she knew no one would care, the only decent people in the district were sleeping and that included her parents. Even if her screams were heard it would sound like a normal evening in the Bagmada Kaaraan district. With the two brothers grabbing an arm, she felt herself moving towards some stairs that led up the side of the small café, and to where she knew Absame and his brother resided. But then, if that wasn't scary enough, she saw Abdirahim's Toyota Corolla pulling up at the front of the café.

Despite the alcohol they'd consumed the two brothers released Caaishu from their grip, knowing they were in big trouble. It was the two brothers now that were trembling at the thought of Abdirahim Ali, but not only them. Caaishu's worst nightmare had come true and her heart ached at the thought of Chris, who she knew had taken on more than he could handle. The passenger side window that faced them, wound down slowly, to reveal the face of Abu, wearing his beret and a smile so wide.

'What the hell?' The brothers said together.

The Journalists - Congo Rescue

Caaishu was totally confused, but at the same time pleased at not seeing the face she was expecting. But then a smile appeared on her face as she noticed a figure appearing from the driver's side, it was her friend, it was Chris.

He knew the two brother's would be distracted at the sight of Abu smiling at them, so he resting his arm on top of the vehicle as he aimed his pistol and shot them both dead.

Caaishu, with no hesitation at all, ran towards Chris and gave him a hug, the fact she was Muslim didn't matter at all. She then loosened her hug slightly to look at Chris and ask. 'Is he dead?'

Chris nodded with a wink, and pulled Caaishu back towards him. She could hear his heart beating strongly, a heart that she knew was good. Abu then climbed out of the car, he wanted to meet this young woman whom he'd praised for her bravery. Their eyes met for the first time, and Abu instantly knew she wasn't just brave, but she was also beautiful. 'Hi, I'm Abu Hassan, it's a pleasure to meet such a brave woman, and such a beautiful woman at that.'

But suddenly men armed with rifles and knives were coming out of every ally, door, and shop entrance, and surrounding them in seconds. They could see the two brothers Absame and Abshir

Hassan lying on the floor dead. They aimed their guns at Chris and Abu.

Abu suddenly laid his Ak-47 on the floor and raised his arms before starting to speak in Somali. He explained to them all that they no longer had anyone to fear, and that Abdirahim Ali was dead, along with his three main men. He then continued to explain that there was no need for violence and that their president's intentions were good, and that the promises he'd made to improve the lives of the Somali people were genuine. Chris was impressed and could see that his heart warming speech was working, they were actually listening. Suddenly they started to raise their weapons above their heads while they cheered loudly. Caaishu looked at Chris while feeling so proud and so happy that she'd played a part in bringing this about. Chris was proud of her too, and now knew without doubt, she was definitely the bravest young girl he'd ever met.

Caaishu had heard Abu's speech and hadn't taken her eyes off him for a moment. She wasn't sure why, other than the fact he was as handsome as hell, but she knew he was a man whom she could love.

--*Chapter Fifteen*--

CHRIS HAD WOKE up early the next morning, he knew he had a flight to catch, and knew now he could leave with peace of mind. He'd only been in Somalia for one night, but had met some amazing people, the most amazing being a young woman whose bravery had helped a whole community. A young woman he now hoped could live her life without fear, for her, and her family. He'd seen how she and Abu Hassan had looked at each other, and hoped that was where her future was heading. Abu Hassan was a fine young man, who'd joined the SAS to help improve the lives of his citizens, and help wean the young men from the Jihadists that were making their country so hard to bear.

At the corner of his eye, he'd seen someone pass the small, front window to his bungalow, and soon after that there was a tap on the door.

John opened the door to see a friendly face and he was wearing a beret.

'Abu Hassan, good to see you, pal,' they shook hands, and Chris just assumed he was there to say bye.

'Hello Chris it's good to see you too, but I've brought someone with me, he'd like to thank you for doing all you've done, for the Somali people.'

'Well, there's no need for that…' Chris then turned to his left and in the direction of the main entrance. There was a large black Mercedes Benz parked just outside.

'Huh, you're kidding me, right.'

Abu shook his head.

Chris made his way to the entrance, knowing who it was sitting in the vehicle and was being watched my several soldiers standing and hiding at a distance. He noticed the back door was already opened so he climbed in.

'Chris you're leaving so soon,' Abshir Mohamed said, while shaking Chris's hand.

'Yes, my work here is done,' he shrugged.

'Yes, it is Chris, and I can't possibly thank you enough.'

'Thank me, really, there's no need to thank me.'

'Well, I believe there is Chris. Because of you we have a corrupt general behind bars, four jihadists that won't be bothering anyone ever again, and we have a very happy president who has asked me to thank you as well. In fact, he's asked me, and this is up to you, of course, if you'd like to stay a little longer at his expense. He'd book you into the Sahafi Hotel where you could drink and eat as much as you like, and maybe you could do some sun bathing too, I know you westerners love to sun bath, yes.'

Chris was momentarily stunned at the gratitude he was seeing, and as it happened, he hadn't taken some free time for himself in quite a while.

'Yeah, I'd like that, thank you.'

'Well, that's fantastic, I'll make all the arrangements, and you just relax here until I send a car to come take to the Sahafi Hotel.

It was midday by the time Caaishu had seen the black Mercedes pull up outside the Jazeera Complex, she knew who it was for, and was so happy.

The Journalists - Congo Rescue

Chris had felt like a king after turning up at the Sahafi Hotel in a black Mercedes Benz. He'd also felt a little underdressed after arriving at such an expensive hotel in just a pair of jeans, and a T-shirt, and a rucksack over his shoulder. But that hadn't mattered; the staff had been given special instruction, and had gone to all lengths to make him welcome.

Now, two days later, he sat beside the swimming with a small brandy and three waiters seeing to his every need. Lapping up the sun, he'd decided it was about time he called his pal, who he was sure must be back in the UK by now.

'Hi pal, how's the British weather today?'

'I wouldn't know, I'm heading up the Congo River,' John said, with a small laugh that Chris could hear clearly enough.

'Okay, so are you going to explain or am I going to have to guess?'

'I'm on my way to the Shaba province, to have a fight with three thousand rebels. John smiled, knowing what was coming next.

'What the fuck, John!'

'Yeah, a group of South American tourists were kidnapped. I'm on my way to try rescue them.'

'Shit John, why didn't you say something.'

'Well, I guessed you had enough on your plate, what with being in Somalia. What yah find out anyhow? Terrorists, right?'

'Yeah, a small group out of the Bagmada Kaaraan district, but they won't be bothering anyone - not anymore.'

'Good on you, Chris.'

'So John, what's the interest in these South American's, do you know them, or is it just one of those days where you feel like putting your life on the line?'

'I know one of them.'

'Is it a woman?'

'Eh, well…'

'I knew it; you're a glutton for punishment, John. Well, I just hope she's worth it pal.'

'Yeah, me too, pal,' John said, looking at Carlos Oliveira and Jose Ramos. 'Chris, Jonathan told me you were booked to fly home the following morning, so what are you still doing there, has it taken you this long to take out that group, or have you decided to take in the sights.'

'Huh, what of Mogadishu you mean, no, I'm staying at the Sahafi Hotel at the president's expense, sitting by the pool drinking a glass of brandy.'

'Yeah, and this boat trip is being paid for by Nelson Mandela.'

Chris knew he wouldn't believe him. 'Listen; if you need me, I'll be here for a while, so just give me a call.'

'Will do pal,' John said, wishing Chris was taking some free time for himself, he knew he deserved it.'

Chris sat drinking his Brandy with a hint of concern for his friend. He knew if anyone could rescue the South Americans it was him, but he hadn't forgotten that John had mentioned that there were three thousand rebels, and he wondered whether he might have taken on a little too much. He'd been to the Democratic Republic of Congo a few times and had visited the Shaba Province during an assignment he was on. From what he could remember it was a beautiful province.

Suddenly he had an idea; he knew his little holiday was all paid for and was flight included having missed is original flight, so after giving it some thought he was wondering whether it might be possible to change the destination, maybe to the Congo he considered.

--Chapter Sixteen--

THE CITY OF Mbandaka could be seen in the distance as they continued their trip up river. John knew they had a long journey ahead of them, but the journey there was never going to be a problem, at least not for him. For the next two to three days they'd be out of danger, it wasn't until they passed Kisangani that, that would change, and he'd always wanted to take a trip up the Congo River. He reached into his rucksack and retrieved a small, but powerful set of binoculars, he'd heard about the amazing bird life that followed the river all the way up to Kisangani. He knew this wasn't exactly a summer boat trip he was on, but for the next two days, to him at least, it might just seem like it.

As they passed through Mbandaka it was obvious there was a lot of construction work going on, which John was sure must be the new military base, and looked quite substantial. However, John's attention was soon drawn towards the beautiful homes that lined the bank, huge structures standing proudly on at least four hectares of land. John could only imagine what it'd be like owning a place like these and with a view to die for. But his interest soon dampened after he'd concluded that people probably did have to die, just so some corrupt official could own their land. Possibly just another example of what it meant to have power in this part of the world. John pondered on just that as they continued further up river to see the thousands of small huts that were barely habitable and which John guessed must be the worker's homes that would have travelled from all over the country just to build the military base. Most would have had no choice other than to leave their family to work in conditions not fit to live in, and to be paid little money, if any.

The Journalists - Congo Rescue

'Coffee John, Maria said, while standing there with a cup in each hand and standing as if not wanting to get to close.

John remembered the coffee she'd made him while he'd stayed at her place, and knew this one would be just as nice. But when he'd seen it was her who was piloting the vessel he'd almost turned back, and Maria had seen that he wasn't happy. It wasn't because he didn't want her there; because if he was honest, he really did want her there because he enjoyed her company. But it was just too dangerous, and if something was to happen, well, he knew he couldn't live with that, and having spent time with her family too, it was just making it all the more hard to deal with. But as he stood there looking at her standing at a distance his heart melted. At that moment he realised if something was to happen and he'd shunned her, or not spoken to her, it was just going to be worse. 'Yes, thank you, Maria.'

'I'm sorry John, if I'd known…'

'It's okay Maria, I'm just worried for you that's all. This isn't a tourist trip, and there's a good chance some of us won't make it.'

Maria had already suspected he wasn't just a Journalist, she'd witnessed that first hand when he'd taken out Amos and his men, but she was curious as to why he was putting his life on the line for a group he didn't even know, or did he, she pondered. 'I know John, and I was warned before hand, some old guy wearing a funny hat had explained it all to me.'

John sniggered under his breath, he knew she was talking about Harry, but it was the way she'd described his hat that had done it.

'But I needed the money, and well, one thousand dollars, that's enough to feed my family for a year.'

'Sorry Maria, what was that?'

'A thousand dollars, he'd paid me straight away, he told me to give it to my family before we left.'

John contemplated for a while on what Maria had just said. He knew his friend hadn't even been paid himself, at least not yet. After some time he'd concluded that despite all the people that his good friend had conned throughout his lifetime, whether they were bad people or not, he did actually have a heart of gold. He'd known that there was a chance that none of them would be returning from the jungle, but by paying Maria before hand and telling her to give it to her family, he'd have known that at least they'd be okay. 'Yes of course, that's a very useful amount of money, Maria.'

The Journalists - Congo Rescue

'John, if it's not too nosey of me, why are you doing this, why are you putting your life on the line for these people, do you know them?'

'Maria you're a sweet kid and I'm very fond of you, but there are some things that you couldn't possibly understand, so just get back behind the wheel and continue to take us up river, please.'

Maria didn't appreciate being spoken to like some kind of insolent teenager. She took her coffee and threw it over John's boots before storming off and going back to the bow of the vessel where she'd taken it out of Auto-drive and continued to steer it herself. She was so angry and her breathing was erratic, but her heart was hurting. She'd warmed to John back at her place, even though she knew he was probably ten years her senior. But since she'd seen him arrive at the boat in the early hours her feelings had grown stronger, now she was sure she'd fallen in love with him. *But how dare he speak to me like that, I'd just asked a question, that all*.

She pondered on just that, trying to figure out what had triggered such a reaction in him, 'do you know them' she remembered asking. Maybe he did, but he could have just said - she suddenly felt sure she knew - only a woman could have sparked such a reaction.

The Journalists - Congo Rescue

John felt bad about the way he'd spoken to Maria, while he looked through his binoculars. But this is why he'd said to Harry, he didn't need any distractions. He had enough on his mind as it was, with going into the jungle where there were three thousand rebel fighters and a Warlord that had ordered more killings than Hitler. But was it that, he considered, or was it the woman he'd spent the night with at the Welcome Hotel back in Kinshasa. He'd struggled to free her from his mind after reading the note she'd left him, but since he'd heard she'd been taken by the rebels, and been seen screaming and kicking while they loaded her on the back of their trucks, she'd been on his mind ever since. But it wasn't until now that he realised just how worried for her he was.

As he continued to look through his binoculars he struggled to concentrate on what he was actually looking for, the birds now seemed somewhat irrelevant.

The sunset was beautiful that night as small dark flecks, that were actually birds flew passed the orangey background. It was such a peaceful atmosphere with there being no cars and no trucks beeping their horns and roaring their engines. Only the quiet sound of the boat's engine could be heard as it rumbled up river, and the birds making their way home for the night, after a hard day's food catching.

'John.' Kapia said, while waving him over.

'Yes, Kapia what is it?'

'Here, I've prepared a small meal.'

'Oh, wow, thank you,' John said, just then wondering what he was going to eat.

'It's not much, but it should help get you through the night.'

'To right, Kapia, thanks again.'

Kapia had taken advantage of the very small kitchen that was below deck which also housed a small shower room and toilet. As she'd said, it wasn't much, but she'd managed to find some pork steaks, potatoes and vegetables. She'd had no intension of making anything for Carlos and Jose, because she just didn't like them, and Maria, well, she'd just assumed she'd prefer to make something for herself.

'Wow, that's actually quite good.'

Kapia was pleased he liked it 'You're welcome, John.'

Maria was quite annoyed as she watched them eat their meal together, she'd wanted to prepare something for him herself, even if she was that little bit angry with him.

The Journalists - Congo Rescue

John had so many things he wanted to discuss with Kapia, but it wasn't a conversation he wanted to have while they were eating. The main thing being of course, why was she even here, after the obvious hell she'd already been through? But knowing there was plenty of time he'd decided to let her enjoy her meal, while he enjoyed his.

It was 5.00 am and John hadn't slept as sound as he would have liked, and that was because his mind had been occupied by a certain Latino woman, but if that wasn't enough, he'd been beating himself up because of the way he'd spoken to Maria. He rolled off his bench to see Carlos and Jose were still sleeping, Kapia sat at the stern, and Maria was at the wheel.

'I'd love a coffee, Maria,' John said, after approaching her from the back.

Maria said nothing. She didn't have to. The look she'd given John before going to make the coffee said it all. John didn't need to take the wheel, he could see it was in auto drive and knew it was possible here because the river was straight enough. He also knew once they'd passed Kisangani they'd be taking a route that branched of heading north, and would wind its way deep into the jungle and be only about ten metres wide and in places even less.

The Journalists - Congo Rescue

The river ahead was like a sheet of stained glass, murky brown, but as still as could be. John knew that wouldn't last as he noticed the lights of a vessel in the distance, probably a couple of miles ahead but coming in their direction. It was only 5.00 am but once the sun comes up this part of the river would usually be quite busy. The next town they would pass was Mbumba in the Mongala province, a small town that he'd learned had either electricity or running water. John guessed it would be mid afternoon before they reach it.

John sat on the small fixed stool that the pilot would use and just listened to the sounds that surrounded them. Birds singing their early morning songs, crickets and frogs that were in the vegetation and on the river bank, and monkeys that were further away and up in the trees. Very few people lived in this area and the wildlife was thriving. John knew this wouldn't be the case in the jungles of Shaba province, where even the monkeys would be hunted by the rebels and roasted over their fires.

Maria placed John's coffee in front of him and just stood there looking up river.

'I'm sorry, Maria I didn't mean to be quite so cruel, it's just that I have a lot on my mind.'

'A woman, you mean?'

John's head dropped as he realised Maria had figured it out. 'Well, eh…'

'You don't need to explain, it's your business, and for whatever reason you have for putting your life on the line, is up to you too.'

John suddenly found himself wanting to explain everything but was sure Maria wouldn't understand that not all men were the same. Some men kidnapped people for money, some raped innocent young girls, some killed with impunity, and then there were men like him. 'You'd better get some sleep, Maria; I'll man the wheel for a while.'

Saying nothing she did what she was asked. She lay on the same bench that John had used while feeling sad, and brokenhearted. She didn't like feeling the way she did, and wished she could be stronger. She hadn't forgotten what he'd done for her and knew she owed him her life, but the thought of another woman in his life and the fact he was willing to die for her, was just ripping her apart.

Women hah, John thought, as he rested his forearm on the wheel. Soon John could hear the sound of groans as Carlos and Jose as they began to stir. He knew they probably weren't used to sleeping on hard benches.

John wasn't quite sure why, other than thinking about uncomfortable places to lay, but it had reminded him of something he'd read about, and were methods used during World War 2. He'd read everything there was to read on World War 2. War was something that interested him. But he'd remembered a particular method that the Jap's apparently used to punish their POW's. They'd tie them to bamboo tables; the tops of the tables where they would lay were basically bamboo sticks spaced out every six inches and that would have been uncomfortable enough. But they'd plant new bamboo plants directly under the table, and with bamboo plants being the quickest growing plants in the world, they'd slowly grow through the poor souls as they lay there.

He wasn't sure why he'd thought of that, but just thinking about bamboo plants had given him an idea and he now found himself searching the river bank.

By mid afternoon as expected, they were passing the small town of Mbumba. Jose and his associate Carlos, now sat at the stern, Kapia slept, John was still at the wheel and Maria was making another coffee for him while hoping to win his heart. The small town looked more like a village and consisted of maybe fifty bamboo huts that were actually homes, a small brick school, and a small market place where the community would sell goods that had come up river from Kinshasa. John felt sure if he'd blinked, he might have missed it.

To John's right was a small fold away table where he'd opened a map, not because he didn't trust Maria to get them to their location but he just wanted to know how much further it was.

'I've made you a coffee John where would you like it.'

If she makes me too much more coffee I won't sleep for a week. Thank you Maria, just stand it over there, please. Maria, how long before we reach Kisangani,' John asked while still looking at the map.

'Oh, it'll be some time, John, early hours, maybe 3.00 - 4.00am. But I have to say we're making good time, I think the engine in this shabby old boat is quite healthy.'

John could remember Harry saying it was almost new, and now he was learning just that.

'Oh, well, that's good. So, from Kisangani to this point, I'm guessing about a day, eighteen hours, maybe,' John asked pointing to their destination on the map.

'Yes, at the speed we're travelling probably closer to eighteen hours,' Maria said while nodding.

'Are you okay Maria?' He'd noticed Maria was looking a little emotional.

The Journalists - Congo Rescue

Maria wiped her nose on her sleeve. 'I'm fine, it's just that this is where my farm is,' Maria pointed to a place only about twenty miles away from the river.

'Ah, Badumbi you mean?'

Maria just nodded, too emotional to speak.

John felt for Maria and put a hand on her shoulder. 'Is this why you know the river so well, Maria?'

'No, you can't get to my farm from the river, its dense jungle. We were considering making a track, because it would have been useful for getting supplies to the farm, we had the money to do it too, but then, well, you know the rest.'

'Joseph Kabila, you mean.'

'Yes,' Maria wipes her nose again. 'The reason I know the river so well is because I'd sometimes work for a company that would supply the diamond mines, they're here, at the location we're heading to. It wasn't for money, though I did get paid a little, it was just that I enjoyed the river, and still do,' she shrugged. 'I was only young and it was more like a holiday than work.'

'So, your farm and the surrounding farms, they're not actually rich in minerals, right?'

'No, of course not, that's what I've never understood, why would they need to take our farms, the diamond are here,' she said pointing at the map again.

'They're lookout posts, Maria. There'll be rebels based there to look out for government soldiers, that way they can warn Kabila in plenty of time,' John had just concluded this but could see the logic. It was clear this Joseph Kabila wasn't just a mean son of a bitch, but he was also a cautious son of a bitch too.

'So you mean they ruined our lives just so they could use our land to look out for soldiers?'

'Yes, I'm afraid so, Maria,' He felt bad for her and pulled her towards him and held her tight for a while. He felt bad for all the farmers that had lost their land to the tyrant. He was just the type of man that John hated and wanted to kill him more than anything. But he knew he was also untouchable with an army three thousand strong, and as Maria had explained, who would follow him to the end of the world. He'd already figured out why, and that was money, and now he knew where that money was coming from. But there was still one thing he was struggling with, and that was how he was getting the diamonds out of the country. He still hadn't made the connection, with Martina's family being in the jewellery business, and Kabila taking over the mines. Every time he thought about it all he could think of was Martina screaming and kicking as they loaded her onto the truck.

'Your coffee getting cold, John.'

'Yes, of course, sorry, my mind was a little preoccupied.'

--Chapter Seventeen--

THAT EVENING JUST like the previous, a beautiful sunset orangey in colour slowly disappeared behind a darkening mountainous landscape. After admiring the beautiful sight for a while John noticed that Kapia was sitting alone at the stern, in fact, he'd noticed she'd spent most of her time sitting alone.

'How are you this evening, Kapia?'

She looked up at John from where she was sitting, after sitting there and looking at the deck for quite some time. She'd been deep in thought. 'I'm fine, John.'

'You seem to spend a lot of time on your own, and deep in thought I might add.' It didn't need a genius to know she'd been through hell because her face told all. Scars three inches long covered both sides of her face, and were evenly spaced out, which meant only one thing, someone had done it, and had taken his time about it.

'I prefer to be alone these days, John,' she said, as if she was holding a dark secret and wanted no one to know.

'You can speak to me you know, if you wanted.' John knew he had to be delicate because he felt she probably hadn't spoken to anyone about her ordeal - in a place that John could only imagine to have been like a hell on earth.

Kapia had liked John ever since she'd first met him at the Brazilian Embassy, the way he'd spoken to her so politely, and the way he'd put the South Americans in their place. She could tell he was a good man as well as a strong man, and she could tell he'd seen things that no one should ever see, just like her. 'I was his wife, or at least that's what he called me. I couldn't stand being near him, I hated him. He killed my whole family, just letting my son live so he could work the mines.'

'Your son, is he still alive?'

'I don't think so, he couldn't be, it's been too long, they don't usually last more than two years.'

'But, you'd been held five years, right.'

'Yes, he took me a longtime before he took the mines and the surrounding area. But it was after he'd taken the mines that my family had tried to rescue me, now their dead.'

'Wow, but you can't blame yourself for that, Kapia.'

'But I do,' she said, shrugging her shoulders.

John knew if she did, that was one hell of a burden to carry.

Though Kapia wasn't as distressed as one might have thought, talking about such a delicate subject, and that was because she liked telling John her story even though she knew it was more like a nightmare, she'd wanted to talk about it for some time now, but with her family all dead, there was no one who she thought would understand what she'd been through, John was different, she knew he'd understand.

'So, what about those scars, Kapia?'

'It's what he does; he has at least a dozen women that he liked to call his wife's, but when he's had enough, he does this so no one will want them after he's done with them. Even then he doesn't let them go, there are dozens just roaming the camp, living on leftovers, being kicked and laughed at by his rebels, too afraid and too weak to try and escape, even though they know they wouldn't be missed. He likes to call them, his dogs.'

John thought he'd seen and heard it all, but now realised this Joseph Kabila was one on his own. 'Where did you find the strength from, Kapia, to escape I mean.'

She looked at John who was now sitting beside her and said. 'Hatred is a powerful tool, John.'

John knew it was, and it had led him to his last question. 'Why are you here, Kapia, why have you really come, I mean besides showing us the location?'

'Well, it wasn't for the money if that's what you mean.' She cleared her throat, and then spat it out on the deck, she had no reason to behave like a lady, she wasn't a lady, not any more. 'I'm going to kill him; I'm going to shoot him right between the eyes.'

Anger was for sure a powerful emotion and Kapia was obviously consumed with it, but John also knew it can make a person do crazy things, ridiculous things. 'But Kapia, you won't even get close to him.'

'Yes I will, because he won't even know I'm missing, like I said, once we're cast out of his so called family, we're just dogs, he won't free us but no one really notices us, at least not as a person, we're just objects to abuse and insult. All I have to do is wear the same clothes and make it look like I hadn't even left, the difference of course - is that I will be strong and I will be armed.'

John was impressed, and had to wonder whether that might actually work, but it was obvious enough, even if she manages to kill Kabila she won't be leaving the camp ever again, at least not alive. 'That's one hell of a plan, Kapia, but you do know that it would also mean certain death.'

'Of course, but that doesn't matter, I'm only alive today because of my hatred for him is keeping me alive, once he's dead I'll be happy to die and join my family.'

John admired her for her bravery, even though he knew it wasn't that that kept her going. But to relive the nightmare she'd endured for five years, to actually enter Joseph Kabila's camp voluntarily was going to take extraordinary strength. But he felt sure she could go through with it. Just the fact she hadn't mentioned him by his name during their whole conversation had helped him realise just how much she hated him.

The Journalists - Congo Rescue

John simmered on Kapia's plan for a while and made some adjustments to his own plan. As much as he admired and liked Kapia, he would never try to persuade her not to carry out what was for sure going to be a suicide mission; he knew how important it was to her. But he was going to need a diversion while he and the South Americans rescued the group. *Um, that just might work.*

'John, how much do you trust those two,' Kapia asked, while looking at Carlos Oliveira and Jose Ramos.

'Not much if I'm to be honest,' John shrugged

'Me either, so why are you going through with this, you know you'll probably wind up getting killed, along with those two idiots.' Kapia didn't pull her punches, John liked that.

'It's what I do, Kapia, it's what I've always done since I was a young boy; it's what I was born to do,' he shrugged.'

'No John, not this time, there's something more, I feel it,' she knew he wouldn't be going on this mission with people he didn't trust if there weren't something else, something driving him.

John smiled at Kapia, it was a warm smile. 'Get some sleep Kapia I'll see you in the morning.'

John was making his way to the bow to join Maria. 'Hey John, how much further, I'm aching in place's I didn't know existed,' Carlos said.

'Huh, what's wrong guys, haven't you slept rough before, wasn't that part of your training, learning how to survive in the most hostile conditions.'

'Well, yeah, but…'

'We'll be passing Kisangani in the early hours, from there we'll be heading north for a further eighteen hours. We should be there by tomorrow night, that's if we're not spotted and killed before we get there.'

Jose and Carlos swallowed deeply. Neither of them wanted to be there, they hadn't volunteered for the mission, and if it was up to them they wouldn't be there. But it wasn't up to them, their orders had come from the very top, and no more than the Consular Official back in Goma, they daren't disobey orders that had come directly from their President.

Maria was becoming obsessed and now was annoyed that John had been talking to Kapia, and for what seemed like a long time.

'Hi skipper, how we doing.' John liked calling her skipper, just jokingly of course.

'Everything's fine,' she said with a face that would have scared a cat out of his skin.

'What is it now, Maria?'

'Nothing, how's Kapia.'

John couldn't quite believe what he was hearing. It was clear Maria had something on her mind, either that or a very large chip on her shoulder. 'Maria, if you have something on your mind you'd better spit out, because this childish behaviour is really beginning to annoy me, don't you think I have enough to deal with.' John said firmly but not actually wanting to say it at all.

'What, putting your life on the line for that woman, you mean?'

'What would have me do Maria, leave her there to die. There, now you know, there is a woman, I met her in Kinshasa and we spent the night together, but none of that need matter. She and her group are being held by three thousand murderous rebels and a psycho warlord. They'll probably be caged in boxes no bigger than a dog kennel, fed leftovers by rebels who care nothing for them, and they'll probably be wanting to die, begging to die, rather than endure anymore.'

Maria suddenly felt so ashamed, she'd known all along how vicious the rebels were and how cruel Joseph Kabila was, she herself was suffering because of his cruelty. 'I'm so sorry, I've been so selfish, I love you, John, but that's no excuse for my behaviour, I really am so sorry,' she said, with her hand over her mouth.

John pulled her towards him and held her. 'It's okay Maria; let's just put it behind us.' John knew that anger was a powerful tool, just as Kapia had said. But he knew there was something even more powerful and would make you do things even more ridiculous, and that was love, and he should know.

It was 4.00 am and Jose, Carlos and Kapia were sleeping, John and Maria were at the bow and Maria had just made John another coffee while trying to make up for her behaviour.

'Please Maria, any more coffee and I won't sleep, and I will need to sleep before I enter the swampland, you wouldn't want a crocodile to catch me off guard would you.' John grinned.

'Oh, sorry, John, I wasn't thinking,' she said, with just a little bit of a cheeky smile.

The river ahead was covered in a low mist, and the humidity had climbed to at least ninety percent as they entered an area that was regularly called the Tropical Woodlands of the Congo. Kisangani was the largest city in the Tsaopo Province and its lights could be seen ahead. It was a city that even had its own international airport. It had crossed John's mind, and for a moment wondered why they hadn't caught a flight and taken a boat from here. But he already knew Harry was in Goma more than 500 miles away, he knew he was good, but not that good. That's not to mention, the large box of weapons that might just have caught a little attention, while loading it onto a passenger flight.

John suddenly slapped his own arm and then flicked the dead mosquito off that had left a splash of blood, which he then wiped with his hand. 'Welcome to the jungle,' John said, looking at Maria.

'Um, there'll be plenty of those in this area and from now until we return,' Maria said.

John knew there would be, and not just mosquitoes, large spiders, poisonous frogs, and that's not to mention the snakes and crocodiles.

'Not far now, John, the turning should be just up ahead,' Maria said, as she looked carefully, and as she navigated through the mist.

'How long is this mist going to be with us, Maria?'

'Until the sun comes up and then an hour or so, ah, there it is just ahead.'

Maria turned the wheel slowly as they branched off to the right, and headed north, the boat's lights only just giving her enough view ahead.

'Well, if I'm not awake by noon, give me a nudge.' John knew after he had woken, he and everyone on the boat would have to be fully alert, and there'd be no more sleep for anyone.

'Okay, John. John, I should try and find something to cover your face with tonight, the mosquitoes love a handsome face like yours.' Maria said, smiling.

'Ah, I see what you mean, thanks for the warning, Maria,' he said, grinning. He'd noticed the difference in Maria since he'd had a firm chat with her, and was now glad he did. Spending these few days with her had been nice despite her mood swings. He'd remembered that she'd told him she loved him, though at the time he didn't say anything thinking it might just make things worse. He still wasn't quite sure how he felt about Maria. She was ten years his junior, and he'd normally go for the more mature woman. But he knew there was no kidding himself, she was without doubt a very attractive woman.

--Chapter Eighteen--

CHRIS HAD JUST landed at Kisangani's international airport, and was making his way through customs. He'd known John was travelling up river to a place at least sixty miles north of his location, now he had to try getting there himself. His first intention was to get to the river, he'd checked the map that he now had folded in his back pocket and had seen there were no roads going to where he needed to be. He could see exactly where John was and wished he'd gotten there a little sooner as he looked at his GPS phone. He could see John was just ten miles upriver and heading north.

Ten miles wasn't far if you were in a car travelling up a highway, but on a river, he wasn't sure how he was going to catch them up. Chris knew Kisangani was no London, or New York, but he was hoping it might at least show some signs of a modernization, it didn't. As he exited the airport he was thrown into a place that looked as though it had been forgotten, it hadn't of course, it was in fact an ideal city, if you were a farmer. He needed to find a way of getting up river quickly, very quickly, and the fastest means of transport he could see from the airport was a bicycle, lots of bicycles. He did then spot a truck with one head light which was loaded with bananas travelling at least twenty five miles an hour on the road that was just compacted earth. As he stood there looking his hope of being able to help his friend was fading rabidly. If this was the kind of transport they used in the city, he dreaded to think what they used to get up and down the river. 'Oh, shit.'

*

Maria had to reduce the revs and slowed the boat down just a little. She was worried that there might be some floating logs or damaged trees that might harm the propeller, or even the hull.

The Journalists - Congo Rescue

Normally she'd just steer the boat around them, or use a long poll to move them out of the way, but first she'd have to be able to see them. The mist didn't bother Maria; she knew it was normal at this time of year and at this time of the morning. She also knew it wouldn't be just over the river, but would cling to any low lying lands and would be quite the picture come sunrise.

Steering the boat up river here was going to mean her or someone at the wheel at all times. She knew for the next fifteen hours or until they arrive at their destination the river would snake its way through the jungle and even turn back on its self before again heading north. But no matter how many times she travelled its winding waters she loved it just the same. It was somewhere where she found peace and was able to put all her lives traumas behind her.

But she hadn't forgotten where they were heading, and who'd be there living in his secluded hideout. A man who'd taken everything from her and her family and forced them to start again on land that was not even close to being as fertile as the land they owned in Badumbi.

She now felt terrible for the way she'd behaved and was glad John had talked some sense into her. She knew John was risking his life for these people but that was because that was who he was. Okay he'd spent the night with the woman in the group and maybe he did love her, but Maria now knew that wasn't the only reason he was doing what he was doing.

She now realised that she was one of the lucky ones, especially after meeting Kapia. She could have just as easily been captured and held captive or even killed if she and her family hadn't got out in time, okay she'd lost her land, and that was hard to bare, but at least she still had her life and her family too.

At 7.00 am the sun was just beginning to show itself above the mountains up ahead. Birds were singing again at the start of a new day, and frogs in there millions singing in concert, but a familiar buzzing sound around her ear had reminded Maria that the mosquitoes were also singing the new day in, and were no doubt hungry for blood.

Maria soon heard the usual moans and groans as Carlos and Jose, started to wake up, only on this morning the moans and groans where just that little more blatant. She was a little surprised if not a little apprehensive when Carlos approached her at the bow. Just like Kapia she'd never really liked them but realised why they were here and had accepted it. It was obvious enough that he fancied himself and probably more than a little, but as he stood there scratching his face, he struggled a little to bring out his seductive charm that he felt so sure was his forte.

'You'd better put this on your face before you make it worse,' Maria said, passing him some Tiger-Palm ointment.

'Ah, right, yes I think your right,' he said, before going back to where he and his associate had slept.

Maria had almost laughed after seeing his face covered in mosquito bites, but also felt lucky he weren't able to use his charm on her.

The sun had risen and just as Maria had expected, it was quite a picture. The mountains in the back ground, the trees full of birds and the low white mist that lay on the low lying lands. She almost wanted to wakeup John because she was sure he would have loved to see it. But she knew he needed to sleep, and as she thought of the swampland where they were heading, a crocodile swam passed the boat, silent as a fish might be while trying not to arouse it, but deadly as an anaconda that lay in wait of its meal.

'Would you like a coffee, Kapia,' Maria asked now more than before appreciating what she had been through.

The Journalists - Congo Rescue

'No not for me, Maria, I don't drink the awful stuff,' she said while retrieving some ice from the ice cooler box and dropping a couple of cubes in a glass that already contained water. 'So, I get the impression you've met John before?'

Maria nodded. 'Yes, he saved me and my son's life.'

'Wow, he's quite a man isn't he,' Kapia said, while knowing that was just what he was, quite a man.

'Yes, he sure is, I've never met anyone like him, that's for sure.'

'You've become quite attached to him haven't you?'

Maria smiled. 'Is it that obvious?'

'Oh, yeah,' Kapia said, with a couple of quite gigantic nods of her head.

Maria laughed even though she was a little embarrassed. 'Kapia, what happened, I mean with your face an all.'

'Maria, something's are best not spoken about,' Kapia said, not wanting to upset or distress Maria with the story of her ordeal. She knew she could tell John, but thought it better not to share it with anyone else, especially someone like Maria, who she saw as perhaps a little too soft. But despite that the morning had passed by quickly for the both of them as they continued to laugh and joke, and tell stories of their past. Carlos and Jose had wanted to join in too, but felt a little embarrassed covered in Tiger Palm and with their faces full of red blotches.

At noon, as asked, Maria was giving John a nudge to wake him up, but at the same time trying not to laugh. He'd taken her advice and covered his face but clearly hadn't found a sheet, or a piece of cloth, and as he sat up he looked like an Egyptian Mummy with bandages wrapped tightly around his head and face. It took him at least thirty seconds to remove the bandages to see Maria standing there with a cup of coffee, and a huge smile.

'Ah, thanks Maria.'

Maria looked at his face and to even her amazement, saw there weren't as much as a blemish on it.

'You're welcome, John.'

Coffee in hand John went to the bow and was a little surprised to see Kapia there too talking to Maria, especially as he knew she like to be alone. 'Have I missed something here?'

'No, we're just talking, that's all.'

'Um,' John said, while more than a little curious.

'So, how we doing, Maria?'

The Journalists - Congo Rescue

'We're doing fine, John, we should be there my midnight.'

'That's perfect,' John knew arriving during the day had its problems, mainly being seen. But he also knew going through the swampland at night could have its problems too. Crocodiles were difficult enough to see during the day, but at night. 'Maria, pull the boat close to the bank over there.' John had seen something he'd been looking for, and for quite some time. He grabbed a machete out of the boats lockup and grabbed hold a bamboo plant. He'd already removed one bamboo cane and was sharpening one end.

'Hey, Rambo, what yah going to do with that, spear three thousand rebels with it?'

John looked at Carlos Oliveira and scanned him up and down. 'Ah, you'll probably be okay I doubt crocodiles like South American meat, a little too gritty I hear, but I intend to use whatever I can to keep them at bay.'

Carlos looked at Maria and then Kapia, before he looked in the lockup for another machete.

With six hours to go, and the last sunset going down behind the trees before they reached their destination, everyone one was starting to feel a little edgy. Deadly quiet, apart from the jungle sounds itself; they rumbled up river fully alert, eyes peeled.

The Journalists - Congo Rescue

The odd splash could be heard in the river that could have been a crocodile, snake, or just a fish looking for somewhere to hide from its natural predators. John had instructed everyone to be silent at this point, but it was aerie, and very scary.

Both Maria and Kapia had been here before, at night, just like now. They'd heard the jungle before, felt its humid breath on their bodies. Six hours was a long time but the distance was only twenty miles, John knew there could easily be rebel scouts roaming the jungle looking for government soldiers, or anyone they didn't want there.

Carlos Oliveira and Jose Ramos were trying to compare the Congo to the Amazon, they'd remembered how John had compared it back at the Brazilian Embassy, and they now knew he was right, there was no comparison. The trees reached over the river from both sides making like a channel that was leading them to where the swampland was and to where hundreds of crocodiles made their home. They knew if they made it through that, they'd be up against a danger that made the crocodiles seem like small lizards swimming in a garden pond, they'd be up against men. Three thousand strong fighters, armed with an AK-47 and an eighteen inch machete.

'Maria,' John said, quietly. 'Once we've headed into the swampland, I want you to turn the boat around, and keep the engine ticking over. Would you know the sound of an AK-47 if you heard it?'

'Yes, John, it's a sound I'll never forget.' The sound would ring in her ears sometimes, and in her dreams. It was a sound she'd heard only to clearly when she and her family were fleeing for their lives.

'Ah, you mean when you were escaping, right.'

Maria just nodded.

John knew she'd become emotional again so he just continued. 'Well, that's good because if you hear it after we've gone it'll mean we've been seen, and you need to get the hell out of here as quick as you can.'

'But John,' Maria said, her eyes filling.

'No buts, Maria, just put the boat in full throttle and head back down river.'

John then gathered everyone together at the bow. He then discussed the plan with some sadness in his heart after explaining that Kapia was going to create the diversion. But also with some joy knowing she was going to get her revenge, and finally be with her family again.

After the meeting Maria was overcome with emotion and walked away, heading to the stern where she huddled up into a ball.

Kapia joined her soon after. John took the wheel.

Kapia put her arm around Maria. 'It's okay, Maria, this is what I want, this has been my plan all along. Someone has to kill that bastard and it might as well be me.'

'But why, Kapia, why must it be you?'

Kapia hadn't wanted to tell Maria her story, but now felt she had to, she was sure it would make it easier for her to understand why she wanted to do what she was about to do.

Maria cried, and for some time, but eventually she understood that it was something that Kapia did have to do, but she just wished they hadn't become such good friends.

'Maria, Kapia,' John called out, though quietly. 'We're getting close and I need you two to remain at the wheel, you're the only ones that know where exactly we're going. If we miss are destination, we'll end up at the rebels route into camp, if that happens, it'll be all over.'

Kapia looked at the map, and Maria explained exactly where they were.

The Journalists - Congo Rescue

Kapia knew the entrance into the swampland was small and hidden to a degree by trees that drooped over it. But she'd always known she'd be coming back, she remember the vow she'd made just before an old fella picked her up in his boat. 'Do we have a flash light?'

'Yes,' John said, while passing it to her.

Maria had reduced their speed to just a crawl, while Kapia looked for the entrance. There was rustling in the long grass that could have been anything but it was in these situations where the mind would play tricks on you, especially as it was so dark, and so silent, and the fact they knew what it might be. A large fish leaped out of the water doing a back flip and causing Maria's heart to miss a beat. But she remained quiet, she knew she had to.

Metre by metre, foot by foot, they searched the river's bank.

'There.' Kapia knew she'd be back and she'd made her mark to help do just that. She'd had no cloth or rag that she could have tied to a branch, and she'd had no machete which she could have used to remove some of the branches. But the old fella that had picked her up did have a knife, and had wondered why she would go to so much trouble after clearly just escaping the rebels.

'What, is that?' John asked, after seeing what looked like a banana carved into a tree.

'That was my father's company logo.'

John didn't need to ask what kind of company it was.

--Chapter Nineteen--

CARLOS OLIVEIRA AND Jose Ramos were kitted out in camouflage trousers, jacket, and cap, and their faces were striped with black boot polish. Kapia too, though she carried the clothes she'd worn while captive in a black plastic bag that was tied around her waist. John wore his khakis with a vest to match; both his face and arms were darkened using the boot polish. They all had a knife strapped to one leg, and John was hoping that was all they were going to need. But for escape purposes only, they wore an AK-47 over their shoulder and a pistol in a holster that was strapped around their waists.

'Okay men,' John said, referring to Kapia as well of course. 'Grab a bamboo cane, and keep it quiet, crocks have to sleep as well.'

John was the first to climb into the water that was waist deep. Maria had wanted to give him a hug first, but knew this was not the time, and knew she would just become emotional again. Kapia was next, but not until she'd given Maria a hug. Then Jose, climbed out followed, by Carlos, who, while no one was looking grabbed an additional item out of the box that had been enclosed in a smaller box but now hung over his shoulder in a green canvas bag.

They were there and they were gone, like mirages in the night. Maria was left feeling anxious, worried, and terrified for all of them, including Carlos and Jose. But she'd been given her instructions and knew she had to keep it together, hold her nerve, and turn the boat around even though she knew that alone might not be easy with the river so narrow.

The water was warm, and swelled around their waists as Kapia led them ever deeper into the Swamp. Visions of Kapia's escape blinded her view as she remembered just how scared she'd been. She shook her head rigorously knowing that won't do at all, she was on a mission and she knew her family would be watching her, she was not about to let them down now.

John followed close behind keeping a determined lookout for anything moving while being the only one with a flashlight. He knew how clever crocodiles were at creeping up on their prey, just their eyes peeping out above the surface. He also knew the bamboo cane he was holding was no defence, and that it could be crushed by the jaws of a crocodile, but hoped it would at least give him time to move out of its way, or prevent it from moving in for the kill.

Carlos and Jose were wishing they were back in the Amazon, chasing drug dealers and small time criminals. But their orders were clear, and now they were wishing they'd never joined the forces. Even though they hadn't spoken to John much, they'd become quite attached to him. They knew he wasn't getting anything for his troubles and that he was here only because he'd chosen to be. They knew he was a man of integrity and honour, and it was just going to make what they had to do all the more difficult.

As they waded quietly through the swamp, crocodiles could be seen sleeping on mounds of earth that rose from the water and resembled an elephants back. They were just big enough to accommodate two crocodiles though some just the one. Some slept, their eyes closed, some looked docile, but their eyes were open. Some were quite small, but some were huge, and at least four metres long. Lying there like prehistoric monsters, their skin as tough as any armoured vehicle. Even the trees that rose out of the water with their drooping branches looked somewhat ghostly. They continued to creep slowly past the creatures that each and every one of them knew could eat anything, boots and all.

After nearly two hours of wading through swamp water a look of relief shone on all their faces as they saw Kapia finally standing on higher ground, and waving them on.

Once they were all on higher ground they rested for a while, all grateful to still be alive, and not in the stomach of a crocodile.

'Kapia, how the hell did you make it through that lot during the day, or was it at night?'

'No, it was early morning and the sun was up; though with the trees, it's never light, but they weren't sleeping like tonight, maybe they'd gone into the river to hunt for food, or maybe it was because at that time there wasn't much of me to eat, and I hadn't taken a shower for, god knows how long, years maybe. I must have stunk like a deceased rat.' Kapia smiled, even though she knew it wasn't funny at the time.

'Um, that does make sense,' John said.

Everyone looked at John.

'No, I mean the part she said about them going into the river to hunt for food.'

None of them could resist a small smile, even with the precarious situation they were now in, with hundred of crocodiles behind them and thousands of rebel fighters ahead.

'Come on, let's march on, leave the bamboo canes here, it's only about two more miles, that's right isn't it Kapia?'

'Yes, John, though the jungle here is quite thick.'

Hearing that, John wished he'd brought a machete, but he knew the knife he had was no penknife so he proceeded to cut some of the vegetation, making the path there that little easier, but mainly making it more recognisable for their return, or their escape.

They all soldiered on with John up front cutting the path and Kapia close behind giving directions the best she could. It had been more than a year since her escape and well, one jungle looked the same as another.

'This way, John, or is it this way,' she said.

John wasn't so surprised, it was never easy to find the same route in a jungle, hence the reason he was marking the path.

'Don't tell me we're lost,' Carlos said.

'No, we're not lost, Carlos - everyone just remain quiet for a moment.'

They did as they were asked; listening for any sounds other than the sounds of the jungle. They could hear insects of all kinds, frogs, howler monkeys, and even the odd bird that was obviously having a sleepless night. But it was the howler monkeys that could be heard the most clearly, with their high pitched howls that could be heard from miles away. But suddenly it went quiet. John signaled for everyone to get low. Then they heard what they were listening for, sounds that didn't belong in the jungle. Deep, low, voices, and they were coming in their direction.

John puts his finger over his mouth, though there was no need - no one dare make a sound.

It was two rebels and John could see they were walking towards the river at a normal pace, and not having to cut their way through as they amble their way east. They'd obviously stumbled across the rebel's route into the jungle from the river.

They waited a while, making sure the rebels were well gone before they moved on. They'd decided to use the rebels route the rest of the way, but while keeping a determined lookout for more of the savage animals, whom they knew if saw them wouldn't hesitate to use their machetes.

It was 4.00 am when they first smelt the camp fires, and heard the occasional voice. John led them left and off the route, and to where they could see the camp from a secluded place where the grass was long.

John reached for his binoculars that were hanging around his neck, while dreading what he might see. As he searched he couldn't see much at all, it was still dark. Though he could see the camp was huge, tens of dozens of like small wood cabins lye to the left of his position. John knew they'd be for the rebels. But then there was a larger quite nice log cabin to his right that even had glass windows and window boxes that contained flowers. John might have thought that was where Joseph Kabila was residing if not for the place that stood directly in front of him and was huge. But it did leave him curious as to who actually did reside in the place to his right, which had flowers on the windows.

The Journalists - Congo Rescue

Then John caught sight of a large shelter to his right and beyond the nice log cabin. It was supported by large posts, or trees that they'd obviously taken from the jungle. There were no walls as such just miles of barbwire that was keeping something or someone inside. 'Kapia, what's the large shelter for?'

'That's where they keep the workers, or should I say slaves, that work the mines, that's where my son used to be held.'

It suddenly seemed obvious enough now that Kapia had said, and he felt for her loss, but John still couldn't see where they were holding the group.

'Kapia, take a look, see if you can spot where they might be holding the group,' John whispered.

Kapia took John's binoculars while feeling a little emotional, but she knew she had to keep it together as she glanced upon the last place she'd been held captive and where she'd experienced hell for two years. During that two years there had been no western hostages or captives so even she wasn't sure where they might be held. But suddenly she did set her eyes upon what looked like just a ball of material, she knew what it was, it was one of Kabila dogs rolled up on the floor and sleeping in the open. She knew the rest could be anywhere, sleeping under tables, sleeping under Kabila's home that was mounted on posts that held it about a metre above the ground, even sleeping in the shower block that was used by the rebels. It didn't matter that one might walk in wanting to take a shower and would be totally nude, nothing mattered, not anymore, they were just dogs now.

She did know where they put their slaves; the ones they'd decided needed punishing, and she'd heard John mention them on the boat. 'I don't know, John, but they could be behind the workers shelter. It's where he puts the men he wants punishing, if they are there they'll be in small bamboo cages, no bigger than a metre high, just like the ones I heard you describe to Maria.'

'Behind the shelter,' John said, rubbing his chin. He looked around, it was quiet enough he thought. 'Okay, you guys hang around here. I'm going to see if I can get a better view from over there,' he said, pointing to the right on their position.

Kapia wanted to say take care, but she knew he would anyhow. Besides, he was gone before she would have had the chance.

John kept low while he made his way to where he could see the back of the shelter. The grass was long which was good, because otherwise he would have had to make his way on his knees, or even his stomach. He found a place that he thought suitable, before looking through his binoculars. Just as he'd seen before in camps just like this one, men without hardly any flesh on them locked in cage's made of bamboo. It was dark now, but he knew once the sun came up it would be even more despicable than what it was now, not being able to fully stretch your legs, sitting on the bamboo canes, for days, for weeks, and even months at a time, and with the African sun beaming down on you, burning you. John's dislike for this Joseph Kabila was increasing with each thing he heard and saw he knew he was clearly a monster of the highest degree.

But no matter how long he looked John could not see the group. He felt a sense of relief after not seeing them in the cages, that was for sure something he didn't want to see, but where the hell were they? He asked himself.

'I think we've been on a wild-goose-chase, guys.' John said, after making his way back. 'Carlos, are you sure the group was brought here?'

'No, of course not, but according to our intelligence this is the only camp Kabila has, where else would they be.'

'Well, it's clear they're not here, we might as well head back,' John said, then he noticed Kapia had removed the plastic bag from her waist and was about to open it. 'Kapia what…'

'This doesn't mean I can't complete my mission, John.'

'No, of course not, Kapia, but, okay, we'll wait until the sun comes up and see what emerges.'

Carlos and Ramos gave a discreet sigh of relief knowing if their plan was going to work, or their orders were to be carried out, they all had to be there. They were sure they knew where the group was and were confident by sunrise everyone else would too.

John sat watching a string of soldier ants that stretched as far as he could see without actually standing up. He estimated them to be one and a half centimetres long, and in their tens of thousands, as they carried their eggs and food to their new base. Unwavering and resolute, he knew they were an army to be proud of, and would only kill to survive.

The door to the centre cabin opened as a daunting figure appeared. 'Is that him Kapia?'

'That's him,' she said.

Standing six feet plus, with broad shoulders and a chest as big as the Consular Officials back in Goma, even John was intimidated. He was still wearing the army issued attire that was supplied during the war, a war he alone wasn't willing to end until he got what he wanted, which at first was just a seat in government, but now was the Democratic Republic of Congo.

The sun wasn't quite up, but the sky could be seen slowly getting lighter, as a few of his rebels started to emerge from their cabins to the left of John's position, and walk across the camp towards the large shelter. Three large bench tables stood just outside the shelter where the prisoners, slaves, whatever you wanted to call them were forced to sit, while the rebels filled their bowls with food.

John knew even Joseph Kabila would know if you wanted men to work you had to feed them first, but as he looked through his binoculars he could see only weak men, tired men.

The lighter it became, the more hellish the camp became. John had spotted a small pig pen just beyond the rebel's cabins, and where a man was strung up, or at least the half that hadn't been eaten yet. At the centre of the camp was some kind of wooden frame with chains hanging from it, John could only imagine what that was used for.

The sun was now beaming down on the camp as the door to the nice cabin that sat to the right of Kabila cabin opened. John's face turned a deep red as he watched an old adversary of his emerge.

'Do you know who that is, Kapia?'

'Not really, I mean I've seen him before, he often comes and deliver large crates, but I never did know what was in them.'

'Weapons, Kapia, that's what was in them.'

Gabriel Dubois one of the biggest arms dealers on the African continent, a Frenchman that hadn't returned to his home country since he was a boy because he'd killed his own father and has been on the run ever since. He wasn't on the run now, at least not in Africa or the Middle East, in fact, he was in great demand. Now around the same age as John, he wore a neatly trimmed goatee beard, and a quite thick moustache. His hat not so un-similar to the one Harry wore only the brim was wider and more suitable for the African climate. He was the main supplier of weapons to groups like Al Shabab, Bokoharam, and had been known to supply Al Qaeda. But he was a man who could smell a rebellion from right across the Africa Continent, and that was clearly why he was here.

'That bastard, I thought he was dead,' John said to himself, though loud enough for the rest to hear.

'Who is he John,' Kapia asked, even though she felt she should have known.

'An old adversary of mine, but who he is, is not important, what he does, is.'

'Supply weapons,' Kapia said, having wanted to know for some time.

'Exactly,' and John knew he wasn't cheep. In fact, he knew a lot about the man that up until now he thought was dead. He knew he was a man who'd sell his own flesh and blood if it helped line his own pockets. He also knew he was a man who didn't need bodyguards to protect him from the sought of people he did business with and who could travel to places like this unheeded, no one wanted to kill the man that fed them, and he fed them with whatever weapons they needed.

John wanted to march into camp and shoot him in the head along with Joseph Kabila but the hundreds of rebels that were now emerging from their cabins and heading to the shower block, had reminded him that that would be impossible. 'If you still want to continue with this Kapia...'

Then suddenly someone else emerged from the nice log cabin, and it was enough to make John shake his head before taking another look.

--Chapter Twenty--

MEANWHILE, CHRIS HAD searched high and low for something to take him up river and in double quick time. He'd walked down to the river hoping to find something with double outboard motors on the back that could zoom him up river quicker than spider could catch a fly after it had flown into its web. But all he had seen was beaten up old boats that were older than the cars that were now passing him by. He loved old cars and had always been interested in vintage cars, and was sure if he had the right person with him to do the wheeling and dealing he was sure he'd make a killing, which had just happened to give him an idea.

*

John was still in shock and trying to figure out what the hell was happening after just seeing Martina's father appear at the entrance to the nice cabin, and looking as though he was on vacation, and the fact he was talking to Gabriel Dubious as though they were good friends was making his head spin.

Joseph Kabila had yelled at some of his rebels, and now they were bringing food, lots of it, and placing it on a table that sat on a large porch outside Kabila's cabin. Martina's father and Gabriel Dubious were heading that way, obviously about to join him for breakfast. But it wasn't until John saw the real reason he was there in the first place, stretching and yawning and looking sexier than Marilyn Monroe that his head really started to spin.

'Is that her, John?' Kapia said, knowing there was something more that had drawn him here, and while wearing a very slight sarcastic smile.

'Not now Kapia. What the fuck!' John said, now feeling like he'd been suckered into doing something that didn't concern him. He turned around to face Carlos Oliveira and Jose Ramos, but he was too late. Carlos had a sniper rifle complete with silencer that he'd leaned on a tree branch and had it aimed at the camp. He'd fired before John could stop him. 'What have you done!' John looked back around to see Martina's father lying on the ground. 'You fool, you've just killed us all.'

'Sorry John, we had no choice, our orders were to kill Francisco Santos and then kill you. Jose now had his pistol aimed at John.

'You've already killed me, and yourselves, so you can do what you like, but who is this Francisco Santos,' John had to know even though he knew it no longer mattered.

'He's a diamond smuggler and he's embarrassing my government, they've been trying to arrest him for years, but he'd outsmarted them at every turn, now they just want him dead, whatever that might entail.'

'But they were seen kicking and screaming as they were loaded onto to the trucks, it was witnessed by hundreds.'

'An act, John, just an act, to make them look like the innocent party - who'd suspect a group of hostages to be smuggling diamonds.'

Jose suddenly lowered his gun.

The Journalists - Congo Rescue

'We've decided we're not going to kill you John, despite our orders, it was just to make it look like a real rescue attempt, that's the only reason we needed you here, but we've grown quite fond of you. John, what did you mean when you said we've killed us all, they'll never know where the shot came from.'

'You fool, they don't have to know where the shot came from, this entire area will be littered with spy posts, they'll have the whole place surrounded within minutes, we'll never get out of here.'

The panic on Carlos's and Jose's face was clear. 'We're out of here,' was all they said, before heading down the rebel's route again. They'd thought it was going to be relatively easy, kill Francisco Santos, then get out of there as quick as possible, but they'd learned a lot since meeting John Stone, and now they were scared, really scared.

'Come on Kapia, we need to get out of here now.'

'I can't go with you, John.'

'What do you mean you can't go with me, you'll never make it back into camp, those two idiots have seen to that.'

'It's not that, John.'

'Then what is it.' Kapia looked as if she'd seen a ghost, John hadn't seen her with such a look on her face.

While John had been talking to Carlos, Kapia had been looking through John's binoculars; she'd seen someone she'd thought was dead. 'My son, he's still alive.'

John understood how she felt, but knew this meant she had to stay alive more than ever. He grabbed her by the shoulders and shook her rigorously. 'This is why we have to go, if you want to help your boy you have to remain alive, you're no use to him dead, Kapia.'

She looks up at John.

John looks into her eyes. 'I promise you we'll be back, Kapia, but now we have to go, right now.'

Kapia trusted John and soon after, with John's help, she lifted herself onto her feet.

'That's my girl, let's get out of here.'

John took one last look into camp to see Martina Gomez kneeling over her father. John now knew, she wasn't the person he'd thought she was when he'd first met her at the bar in Kinshasa. Now he knew she was a mean, callous woman, only looking to line her pockets despite what she'd seen in the very camp she resided in.

The Journalists - Congo Rescue

Joseph Kabila could be seen howling at his men has they headed towards John's position in their thousands, waving their machetes high in the air.

Gabriel Dubois was looking pissed too, waving his arms in the air frantically.

John and Kapia ran for their lives, first using the rebel's route out of camp until John saw his mark, where he knew he had to go left. But he could see tracks, boots, Carlos and Jose's tracks, they'd gone straight on. 'Bloody idiots, he said to himself.'

The soft, ground shook, as the voices of thousands of rebels could be heard coming from all directions like a cattle stampede moving ever closer. It wasn't long before they heard the screams and squeals of Carlos and Jose. John understood they were under orders, and had to do what they had to do, and appreciated the fact they hadn't killed him, though at the same time wondering whether that really mattered, at least a shot to the head would have been quick.

Kapia was leading the way and was pleased John had marked the path. She was now more determined to live than even before when her hatred for Kabila was the only thing keeping her alive, it wasn't him now who she wanted to live for. They jumped into the swamp water while not even given the crocodiles a second thought, and as they waded waist deep, they prayed that the rebels wouldn't follow. They soon realised their prayers had not been heard as shots were fired, and bullets skimmed passed them.

Suddenly there were yelps and screams, and the sound of frantic splashing, a sound that could only have been the rebels being attacked by the crocodiles, maybe their prayers had been heard, but slowing down was not an option. John had remembered he'd told Maria to go if she heard the sound of an AK-47 and he was hoping she'd listened as bullets were again skimming past them and splashing into the swamp water. He felt sure they'd come to the end of the line and it was only a matter of time before they were hit.

But then out of the blue a figure rose from the water and looked like some kind of swamp monster, with swamp-weeds hanging from its head and arms. A whole magazine was emptied into the rebels that had almost caught them and almost killed them. It was Maria, and she was shaken persistently while with her finger still on the trigger of an AK-47.

'Oh my god, Maria!' Kapia said.

John took the gun from her while wanting to hug and kiss her so much, but knew they were not out of trouble yet. They clambered onto the boat as quickly as they could, and Kapia put it into full throttle. John was sure it wasn't going to be enough and as he put a new magazine in the AK-47 that Maria had used, he knew they could cut them off down river. But as he glanced toward the stern for now he was more concerned about the two rebel boats that were coming up from behind. John thanked his good friend Harry as he untied and removed the plastic sheet from the fifty calibre machine gun. Arms, legs and even heads soon penetrated the water's surface as John cut them to pieces, and as the crocodiles eat their remains.

John could see Maria was sitting on one of the benches they used to sleep on and could see she was still shaking. He wanted to comfort her, to console her so much, but knew he had to keep his eyes peeled on the river bank.

It was about one mile downriver and just passed the swamp when it started again. Bullets sprayed the boat as they came from the dense vegetation. 'Get down,' John said, as he fired back but could see nothing. Hundreds of small holes of light appeared in the side of the boat as Kapia and Maria clung to the deck. John was doing his best to fight them off but knew his best was not going to be good enough, especially once they started to use RPGs. It was just as if they were in a heavy rain storm as the bullets clanged and penetrated the boat relentlessly.

But then John could hear a new sound, and it was a familiar sound. He was sure it sounded like an AH-6 helicopter gunship; one of the smallest gunship there was, but extremely aggressive with its twin fifty calibre machine guns and missile capability. *But it couldn't be, could it*, John thought. In no time at all the river bank as a ball of flame and rebels could be heard screaming to the sound of the fifty calibre machine guns. John looked up to see the roundish object hovering above him and with his good friend Chris at the controls.

'Come on girls, we don't want to keep the taxi waiting.' John knew his good friend could hover that machine easier than a humming bird could hover while extracting pollen from a flower.

John helped Maria and Kapia into the two seats at the back of the small but nimble gunship while Chris held it there as though it was being suspended by a crane and not actually flying at all. Chris then brought the passenger side around as John climbed in too, though John did have to wonder where and how Chris had managed to acquire a helicopter gunship deep in the Congo Basin.

The Journalists - Congo Rescue

'John, we don't have much fuel, we can probably only travel about twenty miles.' Chris said, after John had put on his headset.

'Head west to Badumbi, there's a farm there, it belongs to one of the girls sitting in the back, it's about twenty miles.'

'Okay, Badumbi it is.'

John had told Maria they were heading towards her farm and had asked her to keep a close look out for it. Either her or Kapia had seen the Congo Basin from the air and was now appreciating just how beautiful it was as it stretched as far as the eye could see. Kapia was enjoying the ride as they hovered somewhat unsteadily in the little gunship that resembled a bumble bee, in shape anyhow. Even though her heart was with her son whom she'd glanced upon with eyes opened wide and with a feeling of pure shock and bewilderment.

Maria was happy to be flying away from the rebel camp, but she wasn't so keen to be on a helicopter no bigger than a small car that was hovering above familiar land at about two thousand feet, and the sooner she could put her feet on solid ground the better she knew she'd feel. 'There! Down, there,' Maria said, and just before a warning light appeared on the dashboard and an audible alarm rang in their ears. 'What's that John,' Maria shouted, so he could hear through the sound of the helicopter's engine and alarm.

'Oh, that, that's nothing, I wouldn't worry about it,' John said, giving hand signals to help her understand through the noise. But John knew better, and was glad to see they were approaching Maria's farm.

Then suddenly, though not so surprisingly, three rebels stormed out of the farmhouse, and one of them was armed with an RPG.

'Have you got this Chris?'

'No problem, pal.'

They were no match for the gunships machine guns and Chris had cut them down even before the one man could fire his rocket propelled grenade.

The helicopter by now had run out of fuel and was sputtering, and spitting like a badly behaved kid, but somehow Chris managed to land it smoothly enough.

'Wow, I didn't realise helicopters made so many strange noises, Maria said, while now in total quietness after the engine had stopped.

John and Chris looked at each other and laughed out loud.

'What, what did I say,' Maria said, with a smile, and while she looked out the window at her farm.

The Journalists - Congo Rescue

'I'll be there in a while,' John said, as he watched the rest of them enter the farmhouse. He needed some time alone to think, he couldn't remember at any time being taken for such a fool. He could see now why it had been so hard to make the connection between Martina's jewellery business and the diamond mines. It was because he'd been seeing them as the innocent party, just a group that had been snatched by a ruthless warlord. 'How wrong was he,' he said to himself while kicking the helicopters front wheel again and again.

--Chapter Twenty one--

'**WELL, ARE YOU** going to tell me or am going to have to guess, Chris.'

'Ah, that little baby sat outside, you mean. Well, that's a long story, but the short version is, Harry paid a man, who paid another man to steel it for me.'

They both laughed out loud.

'But apparently there's a small military base hidden within the airport in Kisangani, the guy who'd stole it said it was the only helicopter there, and he'd asked if it was suitable for my needs, I told him it was more than suitable.'

'Huh, I bet you did, Chris.'

Again, they both laughed out loud.

'What…is the matter with you two,' Maria asks, while almost wanting to laugh herself, but didn't know why, because she had no idea why they were laughing.

'It's nothing we're just talking about an old friend of ours, you met him, the old fella with the funny hat, remember.'

Maria just nodded and smiled while trying to prepare a meal with what she had. She'd managed to catch a couple of small chickens that were roaming the land freely after escaping their coop that was now in pieces thanks to the rebels.

'Well, we must owe that old bugger a small fortune and I'm not quite sure how we're going to pay him back.'

'Ah, for the gunship you mean.'

'Not just the gunship, Chris, he'd paid someone to steal the boat we were in too, not to mention he'd paid Maria a thousand dollars to pilot it.'

'Yeah, he's quite a diamond that's for sure.'

Diamond, diamonds, John thought he might have an idea as it rattled inside his head.

'Well, I don't see that asshole back in Goma paying him, not considering what he had planned for me.'

'What do you mean, John?'

John then went on to explain the whole sorry saga, and how he'd been suckered into something that never concerned him, and that he'd only been there to make it look like a failed rescue mission. He was going to tell him about Martina, but had decided against it; he felt he'd embarrassed himself enough as it was.

'Those bastards, you wait, I'll kill that son of a bitch.'

John knew Chris was talking about the Consular Official.

'Don't worry about him, Chris; I'll be paying him a visit later.' But John knew they had more pressing concerns, and that didn't include rescuing the rest of the group, even though he felt sure they were probably in immediate danger now that Martina's father was dead.

Kapia sat on the floor, her back leaned up against the wall and her knees bent with her arms resting on them - she was deep in thought.

'How are you doing, Kapia?' John asked, has he rested her hand on the palm of his, and rested his other hand on top.

The Journalists - Congo Rescue

'I'm a little shocked, and a little ashamed I guess,' she said as she looked at John who was kneeling in front of her.

'You have nothing to be ashamed about, Kapia, you thought your boy was dead, and you said it yourself, they don't usually last longer than two years, how was you to know any different.'

'I don't know, John, it's just that when I saw him….' Tears run down her face.

'It's okay, I promise.'

'But he looked so weak, John, how could he have lasted this long.'

John almost wanted to cry himself knowing what she must be going through. 'You need to stay strong just a little longer, I need time to plan, and then we'll be heading back to rescue your boy, or die trying.'

Kapia removed her hand from John's and held both his cheeks. 'You're a good man, John, and I know you'd risk your life if you thought it meant you could save my boy, but really, what hope is there, there's thousands of them, you're just two, what could you possibly do.'

'Have faith, Kapia, you'd be surprised what just two of us can do, besides, we're four, didn't you see Maria, didn't you see what even a young farm girl can do. I thought for a moment there, we were staring in a movie, what was it called? Rambo, I think.'

Kapia laughed while she sniffled and wiped her hand on her sleeve. 'She was great, weren't she.'

'*Yes she was.*' John thought.

'That's better, come on, let's go eat.'

After John and Kapia had joined Chris at the table, Maria placed their meals in front of them. She tried not staring but it wasn't easy. She'd thought in John she'd seen an angel, an avenging angel, and was sure there could be no one else like him, but now she stood looking at two of them, both as handsome as one another, and they were about to eat at her table. 'It's not much, but it should help until I can find something more to eat.'

'That looks okay to be,' Chris said. 'I bet you're quite the cook, when you have what you need, I mean.'

Maria felt her cheeks warming as she blushed, and was glad her skin was dark. 'I do alright, but my grandmother's the cook in our house, and quite a cook she is too.'

'Um, and I can vouch for that,' John said.

After their meal they continued to chat for a while, mainly so the women could get to know Chris a little better, but it hadn't taking long before both, Maria and Kapia had realised they were just alike, in almost every way, only in appearance could they be separated.

Then John's phone rang, it was Harry.

'Harry, it's good to hear from you, pal, what's up mate.'

'John, those two South Americans you're travelling with, they're not to be trusted.'

John frowned, while being a little puzzled. 'How'd you know Harry?'

'Well, I'd been out doing a little business, but when I returned, luckily, I caught sight of two men outside my door, I backed up a little so they couldn't see me - they were armed, John.'

'Shit, those South American bastards,' John said, out loud. 'But you're okay, right, Harry.'

'Yes, I'm just fine; I was more worried about you chaps.'

'We're fine, Harry, everyone is fine.'

'The South Americans?'

'Their dead, Harry, the rebels got them. There's no need for you to concern, everyone here is fine. Harry, you need to get out of Goma, and get yourself somewhere safe.'

'Oh, that's good to hear; I never did like South Americans, already packed and sitting in a car ready to leave for Kinshasa.'

'Sitting in a car, pal?'

'Yeah, I had someone steel it for me, nice too, I have to say.'

John smiled. 'Okay, pal, that's great, you take care on that track to Kinshasa; you know what its like.'

'Will do John, and say hello to Chris won't you. Oh, I presume he got what he was asking for, only he said he needed to get up river in a hurry.'

'The helicopter you mean?'

'Yes, I hope it wasn't too much, only he didn't give me much time.'

'No, Harry it wasn't too much, it was perfect,' John said, while winking and smiling at Chris.

'Oh, that's good.'

'Okay, Harry, you take care now.'

'I will, bye.'

'Those bastards only tried to kill Harry.'

'Is he okay, John,' Chris asks.

'Yeah, he's okay,' John was fuming and was now looking forward more than ever to getting back to Goma. It was obvious enough to him why they wanted Harry dead; he was the only one that knew it was the consulate who requested his help. John was sure by now they'd know their men were dead, and probably weren't too surprised. He was also sure they'd be celebrating thinking it was a successful, failed rescue mission, and the fact that their men were now dead along with everyone else wouldn't have mattered a hoot.

That evening just before sunset, John looked out the window and saw Maria just standing there looking at her farm. His hand rested on her shoulder as he joined her and said. 'It was a very brave thing you did today, Maria, and I'm very grateful. You saved our lives; you do know that, right.'

Maria turned her head so John could see the side of her face. 'Well, I guess we can call it even then, hey John.'

'But why did you not do as I instructed?'

Maria turned and faced John. 'I couldn't do it, John, I tried believe me i….'

Their lips met for the first time as they embraced tightly. John now, not quite sure why he hadn't chosen to do this before, other than having his mind occupied by a certain Latino woman of course. Maria couldn't be happier as she led John into a small barn that sat just to the left of the house. There they spent the night with the pigeons and the occasional field mouse after the door had been open for so long, but that didn't matter, nothing mattered as long as they were together.

The next morning the sun shined through the barn doors and looked like the gates to heaven, but both of them felt grateful that they hadn't been called yet, knowing just how close it had been.

'Wow, where'd you two sleep last night?' Chris asked, embarrassing Maria just a little and unavoidably noticing they were covered in pigeon shit.

Maria disappeared into the shower room. 'None of your business pal,' John said, while smiling. 'Chris we need to put our heads together and come up with a plan to rescue Kapia's boy.'

'That's it, we're just going to rescue Kapia's boy.'

John could see Chris had been busy, and had unfolded his plan and laid it out on the table.

'Now correct me if I'm wrong, but the way I see it, this Kabila guy is dependent on the diamonds to fund his little rebellion. And this South American guy, what was his name?'

'Francisco Santos.' John reminded him.

'Yeah, him, well, he's dead, so now Kabila has no way of getting the diamonds out of the country. Unless he trusts this guy's daughter, Martina, that's right isn't it.'

'Yes, Martina, but that's unlikely.' John said. He was now sure that Kabila would have dealt with Francisco Santos for years now, and they would have built up a relationship, there was too much at stake, billions in diamonds, he wasn't about to let just anyone smuggle them for him, especially an inexperienced woman. It was obvious enough to him now that the only reason there was five of them was simply because the more there were the more they could take out of the country.

'I agree, so, he's already probably panicking, because he'll need the money to buy weapons.'

'Um, there's something I forgot to mention.'

'So, what, is it, John?'

Gabriel Dubious was without doubt an adversary of his, but even more so Chris's. John could still remember the knife fight they'd had in Libya, and the jihadists just turning up in time to save their man, and he and Chris just managing to escape with their lives. They'd had the fight because Gabriel had just killed a good friend of Chris's. 'Gabriel Dubious was at the camp, Chris, and apparently he's been supplying weapons to him for some time.'

'So, when exactly were you going to mention this minor detail, John?'

'Sorry, pal, I didn't want to get you all wound up,' John said, now noticing Chris's fists were clenched.

Chris sat back in his chair while weaving his hands through his long blond hair. 'This mission is getting somewhat exciting hey, John.'

'Don't let it distract you from the mission at hand, that's why I didn't want to tell you, besides, whether they have weapons or not doesn't matter if Kabila can't pay his men.'

Chris leaned forward again.

'Exactly, John, and it's my guess Gabriel, is somewhat pissed too, because he never asks for money up front, it's a policy of his.'

John could remember seeing him waving his arms about, and he did look somewhat pissed. 'Yes, I believe you're right, Chris.'

'Okay, this is the camp.' Chris had drawn a sketch of the camp, or at least an outlined sketch which was just how John had remembered it.'

'And the...'

'Wait a moment, Chris, how'd you know what the camp looked like, you haven't even seen it.'

'Google earth, John, oh, John, you really should keep up with the times, pal.'

'Oh, right, Google earth,' John mattered, but not having a clue what it was.

'Now this is an area about a mile east of the camp, I'd noticed a small area here where we could land the helicopter.'

'Google earth, right.'

'Yes, John.' Chris said, while shaking his head. 'So let me give you the short version first, John. We land here, then, travel west to the camp, we free Kapia's boy and the rest of the workers, then Maria or Kapia or both, can lead them away from the camp via the route we came. 'Are you following me, John?'

'Yes, Chris, but the rebels could catch up with them in a second.'

'Yes, John, once they know they've gone, escaped, which I agree won't take long, they could in fact catch up with Maria, and Kapia, in a second.' Chris pauses just for a second. 'But my point is we blow up the mines.'

John sat silent, while looking at Chris's drawing.

'But don't you see, John, if we blow the mines, Kabila will have nothing, and the rebels will see that, they've already seen their means of getting the diamond out of the country vanish in front of their eyes, blowing up the mines will convince them their wasting their time, they'll know no money is coming. They'll leave in their hundred - thousands.'

John remained silent, though with his head nodding slightly. 'You know there are some floors to your plan, though, right, Chris.

'Yeah, but…'

'Explosives, we'll need plenty.'

'Of course, but they'll have explosives, that's how they work the mines, they'll need plenty.'

'This Google earth, can it point out exactly where the explosives are kept?' John was kidding.

'Eh, no it can't do that…'

'Can it tell you how many guards will be on duty, and how many will actually be guarding the explosives?'

'No, John.'

'Will it tell you how to remove the chains from the shelter's gates without making a sound?'

'No.'

'Um, I like it, Chris.'

Chris smiles, while feeling proud of his plan.

'But there is just one major problem that might have escaped you, Chris. The helicopters out of fuel and somehow I doubt the local garage will sell jet fuel.

'Um, that does present a bit of a problem, John.'

'Kapia and I are going to search for something to eat, we won't go far.'

'Make sure you don't, and if there's a problem, use this.' John passed Maria a small pistol that he'd taken of one of the dead bodies that lay outside.

Maria tucked it down the back of her jeans before leaving with Kapia.

'Beautiful woman, John.'

'Yes, she is, but it's taken me up until now to realise just how beautiful.'

--*Chapter Twenty Two*--

KABILA SAT EATING his breakfast and had eaten his breakfast the day previous, despite what had happened, and despite the fact that the body of Francisco Santos's body lay dead at the bottom of the stairs that led up to his porch. He couldn't think on an empty stomach, and he had plenty to think about. Gabriel Dubois was sitting there enjoying his eggs and bacon, though feeling a little pissed at the events that had taken place. He'd known Francisco Santos for some time and trusted him to sell the diamonds and return with the money so he could then be paid by Kabila, but now he was dead, which meant he had to trust Kabila to find a way of paying him, he was not a happy man. Kabila had had his rebels bring the remainder of the group to his porch, but this time it wasn't to join him for breakfast. He spoke in a very low, deep voice. 'So, who do you think did this, Martina Gomez?' Kabila said, though the Martina Gomez part he'd said real slowly. He knew things about her father, who wasn't actually her real father, that even Martina, didn't know.

'It most probably would have been something my government planned; they've been after him for some time now.' Martina said, she was a strong hearted woman but even she was struggling to keep it together.

'No, not that, we got the two Brazilians, their strung up for my pigs to eat, I'm guessing they'll add some interesting flavours to the pork. No, I'm talking about the other two, they looked like Europeans my guess is they were British. My rebels got a good look at one of them, and they described him as good looking, tanned, and with his hair combed back, he also wore khaki coloured trousers. The other, the one that flew that helicopter and killed at least twenty of my men, had long blond hair. Do any of these descriptions ring a bell?'

The Journalists - Congo Rescue

Martina was about to speak when Gabriel interrupted. 'I know these men. They're a couple of bloody Journalist's. What the hell are they doing here?' Gabriel looks worried.

Martina's mind was working overtime.

Kabila was confused. 'You'd better explain why you look so worried about a couple of Journalist's, Gabriel.'

'Well, you've seen what they can do; they're not just Journalist's, their ex-Special Forces. It's John stone, and Chris Jones. They've been a thorn in my side for as long as can remember.'

'So, you know these two, well, hey, Gabriel?'

'Know them, I should say, I was nearly killed by one of them, and if it wasn't for the people I was doing business with at the time he would have killed me. There was fifty of them, and it wasn't until sometime later I learned they'd all been killed.'

'Killed, killed by whom?'

'The two crazy bustards I just mentioned, John Stone and Chris Jones.'

Kabila wasn't worried; he knew three thousand was a lot more than fifty, but as Gabriel had said, he had seen what they can do, and what they were capable of. 'Martina, do you know these men, and why they've decided to pick a fight with me?'

'No, of course not, Joseph, I've never heard of these men.'

'Well, that is a shame; I guess that means I no longer have a use for you.'

'But Joseph, of course you do. You can trust me. I know all my father's contacts. Nothing needs to change.' She didn't of course, but she knew lying was her only hope, she was well aware of what the alternative might be.

'Know all his contacts did you. You didn't even know your own father, if you did you'd know that he killed your real father, over a dispute about money, though maybe not, you were just a child.'

Martina felt hurt at his accusations, even though she had no idea what he was talking about. Francisco Santos was her father and the only father she could remember. He'd taught her everything she knew, and not just the jewellery business. She knew he was an ambitious man and had always told her if you needed things in life you had to take them, no matter what that entailed. She'd trusted him at his word, she'd seen the slums that sat outside her city's, and the street kid that slept in the gutters. But she did have to wonder why he would say such a thing, and he didn't seem to be a man who liked to make up stories. 'That's just nonsense, Francisco Santos was my father.'

Kabila just laughed, knowing she will never know the truth, not now, not now Francisco Santos is dead. But he did wonder whether he might have a use for her after all. 'Take those three and put them in the cages.'

Francisco Santos's brother and the other two friends said nothing as they were taken away. 'Martina, I think I might have a use for you after all. Take her and get her ready for me, and scrub her well, I hate how those South Americans seem to smell.'

'Yes boss,' his rebels said, now looking forward to their new task.

Gabriel remained sitting as he grinned at Martina while the rebels forced her into Kabila's cabin, though he was impressed to see she wasn't screaming like he'd seen so many others do.

'Double the guard and inform all lookout posts to keep their eyes opened for two westerners, one with long blond hair. Tell them that I want them alive.'

Gabriel didn't think that was wise, but decided to say nothing. He had enough problems knowing he hadn't been paid yet for the last two shipments of weapons, the last thing he needed to do was annoy Kabila now.

As the rebels ripped off Martina's clothes there was just one thing keeping her from grabbing one of their knives and ending her own life. Of course she knew the men that Kabila had described, well, one of them in any case. He was a man she'd often thought about since she'd spent the night with him in Kinshasa. She often recalled how gentle he was with her and how he'd handled her with such care. But she had no idea who he really was, not until Gabriel had described him with such fear in his eyes. He was obviously not just the gentle man she'd remembered, he was also a man that was willing to take on the most feared warlord in the Democratic Republic of Congo. She'd seen in his eyes how he'd felt about her as he had laid on top of her at the Welcome Hotel, and was sure the first attempt to rescue her had failed because of two men that were from her own country. But she was also sure he'd be back, and this time would succeed. The rebels threw her under the cold shower while they scrubbed and cleaned her and in places that only a woman should clean.

--*Chapter Twenty Three*--

THAT EVENING, JUST before sunset, Maria and Kapia were out looking for something to eat, while John and Chris were searching Maria's barn for something they could use to remove the chains on the shelter, despite not yet knowing how they were going to fuel up the helicopter. 'Ah, these should do it, John,' Chris said, standing there smiling and holding some bolt-cutters.

'Good one mate, they'll do just fine.'

'So, that's it, all we need now is some Jet fuel,' John said, then sitting down with his hand on his head.

The Journalists - Congo Rescue

'Um, it's a bitch alright; the nearest place is Kisangani and that's about sixty to seventy miles away, and we don't even have a vehicle,' Chris said, while kicking an old tractor wheel.

'So, you and John finally have a thing going, Maria.' Kapia said, after seeing she had a smile on her face all afternoon and in fact, since early morning.

'How'd you know, is it that obvious, Kapia.'

'Oh, yeah,' Kapia said, again, with two gargantuan size nods. But Kapia had become very fond of Maria, and although she didn't show it, she was just that little concerned for her. Her being the elder of the two if only by five years or so, she felt she should give her a little motherly advice. 'You do realise if we manage to rescue my boy, or even if we don't.' Kapia couldn't even bear, to think about that. 'Well, he has a job to do, and you know that job could take him anywhere.'

Maria knew what Kapia was trying to say while being so careful not to hurt her feelings. 'I've thought about nothing else and I would never try to stop him doing what he does. I love him more than I can express, but this is about more than just me. John has helped people all over the world, it's who he is. I would never try and stop from him doing that.'

Kapia had seen how much Maria had grown in such a short time and she'd put that down to her knowing John. She walked up to her and gave her a hug. 'I'm so proud of you, Maria, oh, and thank you for saving my live by the way,' Kapia said, smiling warmly.

'Kapia, I've been thinking, if everything turns out okay, and we rescue your son, and someday I get my farm back, well, I was just wondering if you might want to come live with us, you know you'd be more than welcome.'

Kapia hadn't felt emotion like she was feeling now in quite some time, and for sure she'd love to come stay with Maria's family. 'Let take it one step at a time shall we, Maria, I mean we have a lot to do, maybe it's a little early to start planning our future - don't you think.'

Maria nodded, and it was a nod full of understanding. 'Yes, of course, Kapia, I just wanted you to know, that's all.'

'What are you two looking so miserable about?' Kapia asked after they'd reached the farmhouse, and saw John and Chris sitting in the barn, both resting their chins in their hands.'

John stood up. 'Well, we've come up with a plan, and we've almost got everything in place, but there's a small problem, we need to refuel the helicopter.'

'So.'

'Well, we have no fuel, Kapia.'

Maria picked up a jerrycan; it was what they used to put the diesel in for the tractor. John and Chris both smiled, they knew she was just trying to help. 'No, Maria, it has to be jet fuel, the only place that would have it is an airport or military base.'

Maria could now see why that might be a problem, but was sure they'd come up with something, some kind of solution. 'Hey, guy's, cheer up, I'm sure you'll think of something, look what me and Kapia found.' Maria was holding her cap, and it was full of chicken eggs. 'You wouldn't believe it; the chickens had made their coop in the old plane wreckage just across the way.'

Chris and John instantly looked at one another. 'What was that, Maria?'

'The chickens, they'd…'

'No, the other part, Maria.'

'The plane wreckage, you mean?'

Chris stood up and joined John; they looked as though they'd just won the lottery or something.

'How long has this wreckage been there, Maria?'

'Oh, not that long, a year, maybe a little longer, it's been cordoned off, to stop kids playing on it, I think they were worried in case it blew up or something like that.'

John approached Maria and rested his hands on her shoulders before giving her a kiss, smack on the lips.

'What was that for, John?' Maria asked, smiling.

'Can you show us, Maria.'

'We'll, yes, of course, if that's what you want, but why…'

'I think you might have just solved our problem, Maria.' John said, grabbing her hand and leading out of the barn.

'Oh, I have?'

They soon arrived at the wreckage, and John and Chris smiled at one another after they'd seen the wings were still intact. They'd recognised it as an old Dash 8.300 twin propeller aircraft and looked like it might be one of the first ever made, and they knew the fuel was stored in the wings.

'Okay, you two keep a look out while Chris and I take a look.'

Chris and John approached the plain with fingers crossed.

The Journalists - Congo Rescue

Maria still wasn't sure what all the excitement was about, Kapia thought she did, especially as Chris had brought the jerrycan with him.

John and Chris had made two or three trips back to the wreckage after they'd discovered the wreckage was almost still full of fuel, and Maria and Kapia had done their best to prepare a meal with what they had. But by now it was already 10.00 pm and they hadn't even eaten yet, not that Chris and John felt that was a priority, but after all the trouble the girls had gone to, they'd decided that one more day wouldn't matter, and would in fact give them time to fine tune their plans.

*

Meanwhile, Martina was dressed up like a French whore, and smelled like one too, after Kabila had told his rebels to douse her in perfume, French perfume, complements of Gabriel Dubois.

She knew she had to remain strong, as she looked at him after he'd taken a shower and stood there naked. She'd been with plenty of men, and mostly for gain, and some that she'd found revolting, one more wasn't going to hurt.

'Come here, Martina.'

Martina did as he said, she found him repulsive, but she didn't want to make him angry, she'd seen him angry.

The Journalists - Congo Rescue

After an hour of being abused again and again by the monster, she lay on the floor while Kabila went to take another shower. She wasn't alone; at least eight other women had sat there and watched the whole thing. For them it was a daily routine, each and every one of them wondering when their time would come again.

She'd known about his wife's, and his dogs, and cared no more about them now, than she had before, even though now she'd become part of Kabila's so called family. Also, she had faith, despite the kind of person she was, she did actually believe in the Lord-Jesus-Christ, and felt sure he'd help her rescuer, the man she'd met in Kinshasa, the kindest, most caring man she'd ever known.

One of the Congolese women wanted to help her off the floor and had reached a hand out to her. 'Don't you touch me. And don't any off you think I'm just like you, I'm not like you, I'm better than any of you, you'll see.'

Kabila soon emerged back into the same room as Martina and his wife's, and he was dressed as though he was now about to go to war, or just invade a small village to kill the people that resided there. He wore the usual military attire that he wears most days, with his pistol strapped around his waist, and his machete that rested on his hip. He was a daunting figure if there ever was one, and Martina looked on, while wishing he was dead.

Suddenly, one of his rebels entered his cabin while trying to catch his breath.

'What is it, man?'

After catching his breath and forcing out the odd cough, the rebel said. 'We think we know where the westerners are holding out. One of our posts in Badumbi, there should be three men there, they're not answering are calls.'

'How far is this post,' Kabila asks, his heart full of rage, his face clearly showing how he was feeling.

'Oh, it is at least twenty miles from here, and we would have to cut a path just to reach it.'

It was obvious enough to Kabila that sending a large force after them would take too long and they'd probably be gone by the time his men got there. 'How many men do we have in the area?'

'There are three more posts, a total of nine men.'

Nine men should be plenty, Kabila thought, but he'd seen what they can do and remembered what Gabriel had said about them killing the fifty jihadists. 'Contact all our men in the area and tell them to head to this location, but make it clear, they're not to confront the westerners, their job will be just to watch them and to inform me of any movement.'

'Yes, of course, I'll get right on it.'

Kabila paced up and down though slowly and with his hand on his chin. With them still being in the area, and killing three more of his men, he knew they must be planning something, but soon with his men being able to tell him their every move, he'd be ready. He was now looking forward to meeting these two men that Gabriel had told him about - with fear in his eyes and while in a state of panic.

Martina smiled discreetly, knowing it wouldn't be long now before her rescuer would come and release her from her present predicament, just a temporary hold up as she saw it, before she could continue her ambitions and secure her future just like her father had taught her. She knew how caring John was, and how gentle he was, and she also remembered how he'd fallen for here, and now she could see he was even willing to die for her.

*

Back at Maria's farm, the four of them were feeling satisfied after just finishing an okay meal, especially considering what they had to work with.

Up until now Maria had resisted looking around the farmhouse, and especially her own bedroom, not that she'd minded sleeping in the barn

312

with her hero, she was sure that would be a night she would never forget, even with the pigeon phoo, and mouse droppings, but it had just been too painful for her. Now she was staring at her bed, and the photos on the wall, while tears ran down her face and memories flashed in her mind. It was hard, but she was determined. She soon started to clean the room and pull the sheets from her bed so she could replace them with fresh ones.

While they'd eaten, John and Chris had told them their plans, which included blowing up the mines, and rescuing Kapia's son along with the rest of the workers. They'd also explained the reasoning behind blowing up the mines, and it had given Maria hope that someday she might even get her farm back. Though she did understand just how dangerous it was going to be, and that anything could happen, and that of course included them all getting killed. But she continued to clean her room even, knowing it might be the last time she ever stayed there, but if that was going to be the case she at least knew she was going to make it special, for her, and for John.

'Kapia, I don't suppose you can remember where they keep all the explosives at the camp, I mean.' John asked, while he, Chris, and Kapia were still sitting around the table.

'Not exactly, John, though I assume they're kept at the mines, I can still remember Joseph Kabila killing one of his men, and it was because he'd brought the explosives into the camp.'

John and Chris looked at one another and had hoped that might be the case. They knew if the explosives were locked up somewhere in the camp, that would mean them having to enter the camp first before returning to the mines. John could now see their plan coming together, each little part connecting like a jigsaw puzzle, all he hoped now was that the picture once the puzzle was complete, would be a picture of them all residing at Maria's farm, and Joseph Kabila being taken away by the new government, either that or him cutting his head off with a machete.

Though the picture in Chris's mind was not of Kabila, it was of Gabriel Dubois, a man he'd tried to kill before, and a man he was determined to kill this time.

John had wondered where Maria was, he hadn't seen her in at least an hour. He made his way around the farmhouse that he was not yet familiar with. It wasn't too un-similar to the place Maria stayed in now, though it was bigger, much bigger. After climbing the stairs and entering a few rooms he finally saw Maria sitting on the freshly made bed and with the odd tear running down her face.

John sat down beside her and placed his arm over her shoulders. He didn't have to ask why she looked so sad, it was obvious enough. 'Wow, this is a lovely room, Maria.' He said, then looking out of the window. It was dark, but he'd seen the surrounding area and was sure the view was wonderful.

'I used to spend hours just sitting at that window, just looking at the fields and crops, watching my family as they worked.

'And so you will again Maria, I promise.' He knew how painful it must be, and wished he could just wave the pain away. But he knew it was going to take much more than that, but he was a man of his word and he'd made a promise, a promise he was determined to keep. He had considered not sleeping at all that evening; he knew there must be rebels in the area, residing in other farms that they'd taken from their owners. But as he now lay beside Maria, just holding her, comforting her, watching her fall asleep, he'd found himself doing the same.

It was just two hours later, when he woke up in a cold sweat, after having one of his dreams. He climbed out of bed and made his way to the kitchen where he knew there was some cool, fresh water that he and Chris had taken from the well just that afternoon.

'Restless night was it, pal?' Chris asked, while still sitting up the table. He was sure it had been, he knew both him and John had their nightmares.

'Um, that's right, but what are you doing up, pal?'

'Well, I thought it better if at least one of us stayed up in case we're visited by some unfriendly rebels.'

'Um, I'd considered doing the same, but fell asleep watching Maria fall asleep.'

'That's okay, mate, I can keep a look out tonight, then catch up in the morning.' Chris had often wondered when John was going to settle down and get married, and remembered John telling him on many occasions that he would need to find a new career first. He'd seen how John looked at Maria, and wondered if this might be that time, and whether his new career might be working on Maria's farm, if they were able to get it back, of course. But he knew his friend well, and had to consider it with some serious doubt.

'Cheers, pal. So, what do you think, what do you rate our chances, do you think we've bitten on more than we can chew?'

The Journalists - Congo Rescue

'I don't know, pal, that's a question I ask myself before every mission, and, well, I'm still here, and so are you, John. Yes, I think we have a good chance of pulling it off.'

John was hoping he'd say that, because he was wondering whether he might have been feeling a little too confident. 'Um, me too, pal. Right, well, I'll see you in the morning, then.'

'Okay, pal,' Chris said, while getting up to go outside.

--Chapter Twenty Four--

JOHN WOKE UP the next morning, and as it seemed he'd more often than not recently, had woken up alone. *Why do they always do that?* He wondered to himself, though with a small laugh.

He made his way to the kitchen, sure that that's where Maria would be, and his assumption was soon confirmed as he saw her preparing breakfast. 'Good morning, my love,' he said before giving her a kiss on the cheek.

Maria was enjoying making breakfast for them all, with Kapia's help of course. It was as if it was a normal day, and all the family was just getting up to start work on the farm. But she knew that wasn't how it was at all, and knew this could be the very last time she'd be cooking a meal, for them, or for anyone. But she soon perked up when Chris entered the kitchen and joined them at the table. She'd seen it before and was seeing it now, two of the most handsome men she'd seen, sitting at her table. Two angels, avenging angel, as she'd seen them, here at their own choice, and here to take down a monster that had destroyed so many lives, including hers.

'How'd you like your eggs, Chris?'

'Ah, any old how will do, Maria.'

'How did it go last night, Chris, did you see anything at all?'

'Nah, nothing pal, a little surprising isn't it.'

John agreed, though new it would probably take a little time before they found them and was able to muster a force big enough to come after them. 'Yes, it is pal, but you'd better get some sleep, I'll keep a look out.' *A determined look out,* he thought to himself.

Later that morning, John and Kapia were sitting outside shaded by the farmhouse. They'd taken the weapons from the three dead rebels and had stripped them down ready for cleaning, though

John had kept one AK-47 ready and loaded just in case.

'So, Kapia, who taught you how to do this?' He'd remembered seeing her cleaning a pistol when they'd first started their journey upriver.

'I taught myself, John, though most Congolese people know how.'

John felt a little daft because he should have known, this is the Congo after all. 'I'll just check in the barn, I'm sure I saw some light oil in there.'

John had found what he was looking for and was just leaving the barn to join Kapia again when he was sure he saw something in the trees about two hundred metres away. It was something he'd seen before and he knew it was common mistake rebels made when trying not to be seen. They'd clean their machetes that they loved so much, but often forgot about the sun that would reflect clearly of them. He continued what he was doing as if he'd seen nothing, and headed towards where Kapia was sitting. 'Kapia.'

'Yes, John?'

'Don't look, just go and wake up Chris. Tell him I said, he needs to wind up the bird, he'll know what I mean.'

Kapia understood instantly, she could tell by the look on John's face. 'Of, course John,' she said, as she ambled back into the house looking like nothing had happened, it hadn't of course, but she knew it was about to.

John knew what he had to do, and that was to bring the rebels out into the open, which meant him with his AK-47 against however many rebels there were.

He knew the odds of them hitting him from two hundred metres away were slim at best, and him hitting them even less especially as he couldn't even see them. Though hitting them was never his intention, he knew how much the rebels liked a good fight and knew it wouldn't take much to lure them out from where they were hiding, whether they were under orders or not. He knew they were well trained and fearless, but disciplined, he doubted it.

Walking slowly he moved towards their location, firing one round at a time to conserve his ammo, while listening for the sound that he'd been so grateful to hear only a day or two before.

Just as he'd expected, the rebels were leaving the cover and protection they had in the trees and were now marching towards him, nine of them, and they were not conserving their ammo. Bullets flew past his head, while he continued forward, now knowing if his pal didn't hurry up, he'd be dead. *Where the fuck is he,* he thought.

Suddenly, and to John's relief the rebels were stopped in their tracks as the little gunship flew over his head. They scatted like mice might after seeing a tractor heading towards them. But this was no tractor; this was an AH-6 Helicopter gunship, with twin 50 Calibre machine guns and missile capability. It didn't take long, all of three minutes, John estimated as their limbs and spurts of blood flew through the air landing in the fields. John didn't need to check he was sure they were dead.

'Bloody hell, Chris, what took you so long?' John asked, after Chris had landed the helicopter in front of the farmhouse again, and gotten out.

'Oh, sorry, pal, it looked like you were having fun, so I took my time.'

John knew he was only joking. 'Well, thanks, pal, hey, we still have it, don't yah think.'

'Yeah, we still have it, John,' Chris said, while stretching and yarning. 'Do you think I can get some sleep now, I mean without any distractions.'

'Yes, Chris, I think we'll be fine now, go get some sleep, we have a long night ahead.'

John was certain they'd be fine, the rebels they'd just killed were obviously from the nearby lookout posts, and were obviously sent to keep a lookout for any movements. It was for sure Kabila wasn't going to send the bulk of his men there because it was too far, and would take too long. However, everything was about to change, and John knew it. Tonight they were going to execute their plans, overall objective - to finish a man that had murdered countless people, ripped people from their homes and put them to work in the mines, held women against their will while he abused them again and again, and just because he hadn't received concessions from a government who felt he was too violent, and felt he was probably insane.

'How, we doing, Kapia?'

'Getting there, John, just one more AK-47 left to clean.

Later that day Kapia had gone for a walk, she wanted to clear her head; she needed to know exactly what her goal was now that everything had changed. Of course, she wanted to live for her son, but after wanting to kill Kabila for so long and knowing that that would mean she would have to die, she'd accepted that and that had been her mindset for as long as she cared to remember. She was struggling to change that way of thinking. For years she'd thought of nothing else, other than how she was going to kill him. It was in her thoughts and it was in her dreams, and now for the past year she had known exactly how she was going to kill the man she hated so vividly. How was she supposed to just change that way of thinking, to go back into the camp, rescue her boy, and leave knowing Kabila was still alive after all he'd put her and her family through.

John and Maria sat at the table just talking when John suggested something that had been playing on his mind all that morning, and he had wondered why he hadn't considered it before.

'Maria, you needn't come with us tonight.'

'What!'

'Well, there's no need, Kapia can free her boy and the rest of the workers, while Chris and I are rigging up the mine with explosives.'

'Yeah, and who's going to watch Kapia's back. I know they don't bother guarding the shelter, but that's not to say there won't be the odd rebel roaming the camp. Besides, I have as much reason to want to finish that bastard as anyone.'

John knew she did, and she did have a point, there could be the odd rebel roaming the camp. 'You've given this a lot of thought haven't you, Maria.' John said smiling.

The Journalists - Congo Rescue

'Dawn right I have, and if you think I'm just going to hang around here while you're putting your lives on the line you can think again.'

'Okay, okay, it's just that I was worried about you, that's all.'

'Don't worry about me, I can handle myself, you saw…'

'Okay, Maria, you're in,' John said, smiling.

Maria smiled too, and they came together and kissed passionately.

'Get a room you two,' Kapia said, after entering the house after her walk. 'What time are we planning to leave, John?'

'Well, Chris and I have decided on midnight, if you remember the camp was quiet in the early hours, and that should give us time to reach there after landing the helicopter.'

'Alright, then, would anyone like some tea.'

*

Kabila was sitting on his porch about to start his supper, but while looking at Gabriel's plate that lay on the table opposite him. 'Go fetch that Frenchman for me would you.' Kabila said, looking at one of his rebels.

Suddenly the rebel Kabila had ordered to tell the men to watch the post at Badumbi approached the front of his cabin.

'Ah, I was hoping you'd come, what's the latest, have they left the farm yet in that little helicopter, or are they still there planning how they're going to take me down?'

'We don't know, no one is picking up their radio, I think they must have been seen. Kabila, I think they've been killed.'

'What do you mean seen, my orders were for them to just keep a lookout!'

The rebel just shrugged, he was just as surprised as anyone.

Kabila was just about to yell at his man again.

'He's not there, the Frenchman, he's not in his cabin.'

'What! Kabila stood up in a rage before heading towards Gabriel Dubois's cabin. He knew he hadn't even paid him yet and was sure he must still be there. He wasn't. Kabila could see he had taken all his things, which was just a rucksack, and a pistol. Kabila had to compose himself and regain his thoughts. He pondered on what Dubois had said about the two westerners. He hadn't taken him that seriously and that was because he knew he had three thousand rebels watching his back, but he'd seen what they were capable of and it had given him some concern. But he owed Gabriel money, lot's of it, and was now realising just how scared Gabriel had been, and was now wondering whether his concern should have been that little bit greater.

But that hadn't been his only concern in past days and since Francisco Santos had been killed. He'd seen how his men were, and how low their moral was, and he knew he hadn't paid them him months. He was now feeling something for the very first time in his life; he was now worried.

Martina had heard all the commotion and lay there now with a grin on her face, and thoughts of the man who was going to be rescuing her soon. She knew he loved her; it was obvious, why else would he go to so much trouble.

*

Maria, Kapia, and John sat around the table going over their plans and even changing things they felt needed changing. John had hummed and hard about something in his head after his conversation with Maria earlier. But not just that, he was also worried about how long it was going to take Chris and him to rig up all the explosives. 'I think it would be better if I join you and help rescue the workers.'

'But you can't, it'll take Chris too long, he'll never finish in time.'

'I know, and that's my concern. I don't think even with my help we'll finish in time, it could take hours depending on how big the mine is.'

Maria and Kapia were a little confused.

'Kapia, I need to ask something of you, and well, if you want to tell me to piss off, I will totally understand.'

'What is it, John?'

John rubbed his hands together while his elbows were rested on the table. 'How would you feel about it if I was to ask your son, and some of the workers to help us rig up the explosives? Only I feel that's the only way we're...'

'I think he'd be happy to help, John, and the rest of the workers too. He's had them caged up for probably two years, and they would have seen many of their friends and family die in that time. Yes, I think they'd be more than happy to help'

'Fantastic, then that's what we'll do. Chris can take out whatever guards there are guarding the explosives, while we rescue the workers, I'll then bring some of them back to the mines, and you two can lead the rest to a safe location as far away from the camp as possible.'

Kapia and Maria looked at one another and nodded.

The Journalists - Congo Rescue

By 6.00 pm Chris had woken up and had seen all of them sitting around the table eating. 'I hope you've saved some for me, guys?' He said, joking of course.

'Yes, of course, Chris, take a seat at the table and I'll dish it up for you.' Maria said, smiling.

'Any more rebels turn up today, John?'

'Nah, I doubt they'll be any more around here, pal.'

John then went on to explain the changes to their plans, and Chris had agreed, feeling it was a better plan.

During the night there'd gone through the plans again and again until everyone knew their role, and everyone was confident they could do it. By the time the hands on John's watch read twelve o'clock they were all kitted up and ready to go. 'Okay, Chris, you'd better wind up the bird, pal.'

--*Chapter Twenty Five*--

Kapia had enjoyed the flight from the rebel camp to Maria's farm, and seeing the Congo from the air had been amazing, but flying at night all she could see was darkness. Maria hadn't liked the flight to her farm, but this she found terrifying. With no city lights to see below and no stars in the sky because of the clouds, it was only the sound of the engine that reminded her they were actually flying at all, though that was probably a good thing.

The Journalists - Congo Rescue

'You're sure you can find the location, right Chris?' John said, speaking through the microphone on his headset.

'No problem, pal, I've already inputted the coordinates into the helicopters onboard computer.'

'Google Earth, right.'

'Yes, John.'

Chris knew he had to travel north, before finally heading south, so what rebels weren't sleeping didn't see or hear them coming. As Chris descended just above the jungle canopy, it was as if they were being joined by a round, alien aircraft flying just below their position, but actually it was just the headlight, shining downwards onto the trees.

'This, Google Earth, Chris, it's like a satellite image, right?'

'Yes, John.'

'And these images, they're updated like everyday, right?'

'No, John there, oh, shit!' Chris had just realised the image could have been a week old, if not a year. He hovered the small helicopter for some time, flying back and forth over the location, but all he'd seen is trees and vegetation. He glanced to his right. 'Over there, I'm sure that's it,' Chris insisted.

The Journalists - Congo Rescue

Chris was now sure he was looking at the area that he'd seen on Google Earth, which was now just vegetation, but there was no choice, he had to land or return back to Maria's farm, he did not want to go back. He'd noticed something different about the vegetation in this area and was now sure it was just long grass. 'I think I can put it down here, John.'

'Okay, pal.' John had also noticed the vegetation was different and was also sure it was just long grass, the question was, how long.

Chris lowered the helicopter slowly as the air forced from the propellers seemed to flatten the grass as he finally landed it smoothly. 'Phew!' Chris said, somewhat relieved to be on the ground.

'That's it, I'm staying firmly on the ground from now on,' Maria said.

'Well, at least the helicopter will be well hidden, hey Chris.'

'You could say that, John.'

'Alright, it's about a mile in that direction,' John said, looking at his compass.

The jungle there wasn't as dense has it had been when they were heading to the camp from the swampland, but John, as well as Chris still cut the occasional vine to make it easier for the workers. It was dark and the usual sounds of the jungle were clear to hear. Kapia's heart beat was faster just thinking about her son, and now hoped he'd soon be free. She had to adjust her shirt slightly; she didn't want anyone seeing what she had concealed under it. Maria was glad now that they were on the ground, and her adrenaline was flowing fast throughout her body, and she also hoped Kapia's son would be free soon. They were walking upwind and could already smell the camp fires.

'The mines should be just up ahead, Chris.' Just as John had said that they arrived at a folk or man-made path, which led north, as well as straight on. 'Okay, Chris, you know what to do, good luck, pal.'

'You too, mate.' Chris said, now heading north.

John knew it wasn't about luck, but it was just something he liked to say to his buddy. He knew it was about training, and knowing your mission, being highly skilled in hand to hand combat, and an expert in weaponry and explosives, he knew Chris was more than capable.

As they were hoping, they'd arrived at the camp from the west and were now keeping low as they approached the back of the shelter. John had seen it before, but it was no less horrific, but Maria hadn't and was now holding her hand in front of her mouth in disgust. She'd remembered John describing the bamboo cages before, and now she could see why he'd been so serious.

John had noticed something different and it wasn't the cages, but what they contained. Before he'd glanced upon men almost naked, and who were just skin and bones, and they were still there now, but now they were accompanied by people who were fully clothed and John was sure who they must be. John looked closer and could see there were three men all looking quite sick. John knew a lack of food and water and being bitten by mosquitoes would do that, but he did have to wonder where Martina was, and he'd remembered what Kapia had said about his wife's. He'd already realised she wasn't the person he'd once thought she was, but wouldn't wish that on anyone.

One of them caught sight of John with the girls, and the look on his face was clear. John puts his finger over his mouth and the man instantly knew why. John, Maria, and Kapia then snuck past the cages and were soon looking at the workers. Kapia looked thoroughly, but there were too many and they were all curled up sleeping, she hadn't recognised her boy among them.

'Okay Maria, Kapia, you know what to do.'

They did know what to do, and they both crept towards the wooden handmade gates, that were intertwined with barbwire, and with Maria carrying the bolt cutters. She soon applied them and squeezed firmly, but she wasn't strong enough, she couldn't cut the 3/8'' chain. Soon Kapia joined her taking hold of one of the handles while Maria held the other. Together they squeezed as hard as they could and eventually the chain gave way.

John had noticed a single rebel heading their way and had to act quickly, while remembering what Maria had said about watching Kapia's back, he could now see she was absolutely right and was glad he was there to help. He stood up straight and approached the rebel as though he was on a Sunday afternoon stroll. The rebel looked astounded to see a westerner strolling through the camp without a care in the world, or so it seemed. John had soon slit his throat, and he now lay on the dirt, dead.

As quickly as they could, Maria and Kapia started to wake up the workers. The smiles on their face and the tears in their eyes had made Maria emotional, but when Kapia had at last glanced upon her boy, the emotion was overwhelming.

'Mother, is that you?'

'Yes, son, come, we have to go as quick as possible.'

During their discussions, John had told Kapia that once she'd woken up the workers there would be no time for kisses and hugs - they would have to come later.

Maria and Kapia led the worker out from where they'd been forced to sleep for at least the past two years, while noticing how weak they looked, but also how keen they were to get out of the shelter. John kept a lookout, but not without admiring the bravery the two girls were now showing.

John was the last to pass the cages as he was leaving and had signaled to the South American men that someone would be back for them, though at the same time knowing, that would depend on the success of the mission. He also wanted to free the Congolese men that looked almost dead as they sat awkwardly in their cages. He knew that would be impossible, and knew it would take weeks before they could walk again, if they could ever walk at all.

John soon reached the folk in the path where Chris had turned and headed to the mines, and now where at least fifty workers stood looking and feeling happier than they had in a long time. 'Kapia, can you ask them?'

John would have liked to have asked them himself, but couldn't speak Congolese. He knew it was a lot to ask of the men whom John had noticed were young and old, and some very old. But as

Kapia spoke, John could see the smiles on their faces, as they nodded at Kapia - their faces were also full of enthusiasm.

'They want to help, John.' Kapia said now full of emotion.

'Okay, I'll need ten men; they'll need to be the stronger and more agile of the group.'

Kapia explained and had soon separated the group into two groups; her son was among the group who would be helping John and Chris. Kapia was happy her son looked so strong, and she'd seen how keen he was to help. But for her, well, she'd rather see him leave with the other group.

Maria led them in the same direction as they'd come while Kapia watched the rear of the group.

John led the other ten men towards the mines, but not before putting his hand on Kapia's son's shoulder and giving him a friendly wink.

At the entrance to the mines lay two rebels - they were dead with their throats cut. John didn't have to wonder how that happened.

Chris suddenly emerges from the mines. 'What took you so long, pal.' He said, in his usual way and just joking as he usually did.

'So, what do you think, is it doable?'

'Ah, well, there's not as much explosive material as I was hoping, but Yeah, I think it's doable, John.' Chris then went on to explain that the mine was basically a hill and continued to explain that what they needed to do, was to make it cave in on itself.

'Well, we'd better get started then,' John insisted.

They soon went to work and John took five men with him, and Chris did the same. It wasn't long before John, and Chris had noticed just how good the workers were at this, and in fact, had taken over the job while it was them who were doing the manual jobs, using pickaxes to make holes were the explosives would be placed.

It wasn't surprising; it had been all the workers had done for the past two years, working every day, and twelve hour shifts. Their hands were blistered, and their knees were grazed and cut, but on this day they worked like troopers, and John and Chris didn't blame them.

After two hours of hard work, and continuous sweating, John was ready to light the fuse, but suddenly felt it wasn't his job, he knew it shouldn't be him who lit the fuse.

He scanned his eyes over the workers looking for one young man in particular. He spotted Kapia's boy and called him over. It was obvious enough what John wanted him to do, and he smiled in anticipation. He lit the fuse which was quite long, but that didn't stop him and the other nine men running as fast as they could. They'd seen explosions almost every day since their capture, but knew none were going to be like the one they were now expecting. John and Chris ran too, but in a different direction and to higher ground, they wanted to see the reaction to their little fireworks display.

'Well, this is going to be one hell of an early morning call, Chris.' John said, feeling a little emotional.

'Yeah, should be quite something, John, though I hope it has the desired effect, because if it doesn't, three thousand angry rebels are going to be heading this way.'

Then, without warning, the earth shook, and the sound was deafening, the jungle came alive with its wildlife chirping, croaking, and howling and a huge cloud of dirt and rock reached high into the sky.

'Well, that should have done it, John said, now taking his hands away from his ears.

Maria had also jumped even though she was now at least a mile away. She looked for Kapia, wanting to hug her after the success they'd had. She walked back past the workers, all the way back.

Maria had spotted some clothing on the jungle floor and knew it was Kapia's.

'Jee's, that was loud, John.'

John took his binoculars and scanned the mines, or what were mines. Now all he could see was a mound of dirt and rock. He knew the mines were not completely done for, and that within a year, people would be mining the diamonds just like they always had, but it was unlikely to be Joseph Kabila, and the workers would be getting a fair days pay for a fair day's work.

John then scanned the camp with some anxiety, not yet knowing what the reaction of the rebels would be. Thousand of them had emerged from their cabins and all waving their weapons in the air. Kabila could be seen howling at them, instructing them, John felt his stomach churn.

Then out of the crowds of rebels, John could see a single woman heading towards where Joseph Kabila stood, she was dressed in rags and walking as though she had no strength left in her body. Kabila had ignored her, to him, she was just a dog. John suddenly felt he knew better as she continued on and towards where Kabila was still standing. Suddenly, John noticed she had stood up straight, and she'd pulled out a pistol and had it aimed at Joseph Kabila.

The Journalists - Congo Rescue

'Holy shit!'

'What is it, John, what can you see?'

John wanted to say, but at the same time not wanting to pull he eyes away. Then he heard the faint sound of a pistol through the rebels yells. Kabila fell to the ground and the camp became silent.

'She's done it. She's only bloody well done it.'

'Who, John. Done what for Christ sake?'

'Kapia, she's only gone and killed Kabila.'

Chris stood in shock. 'Well, that's the last time we'll be seeing her then,' Chris sighed.

But John wasn't feeling quite so negative, especially after seeing the rebels now putting down their weapons, and starting to walk towards the camp's main entrance. 'She's done it Chris, we've done it. The rebels are leaving and they've left their weapons behind.'

Chris smiled, mainly because he knew how happy his pal was feeling, though of course also because it was his plan.'

John reached into his pocket and pulled out his phone. 'Harry, I'm sorry to call you at this time, pal, but how many officials do you know; only it seems that Kabila is done for.'

'Well, that is good news, John, let me get right on it.'

'Cheers, Harry, oh, Chris will give you some coordinates to the location of Kabila's camp, I think they'll be quite pleased to receive them.'

Maria soon arrived after running all the way back. 'John, Kapia's missing, I think she's gone after Kabila.'

John passed his binoculars to Maria. 'Maria's heart melts as her eyes glance upon her friend just sitting there on the stairs leading up to Kabila's cabin, and now being surrounded by women she'd spent time with at the camp. She'd also seen the rebels leaving in their thousands. She passed John his binoculars before giving him a hug. 'It's over John, I can go back to my farm, and my family can go back too.'

'Yes, Maria, it is over.'

They sat down on the grass at the top of the hill they were on, and just waited, taking turns using John's binoculars and watching the rebels leave. It was a fantastic day, and Maria knew it was because of two men she'd called angels, and who she had now become so close to.

--*Chapter Twenty Six*--

After the sun had finally risen, the sky became a mass of helicopters. Some were huge Chinook helicopters that could carry forty five men, and there were attack helicopters, all armed with missiles and large calibre machine guns. But none were as small and agile as the little gunship that had brought them there, and rescued them, only days before.

'Shouldn't we go down into the camp and fetch Kapia, John?' Maria asks.

The Journalists - Congo Rescue

'Yes, why not, Maria, it should be safe enough now I think.'

They were soon walking into camp and it was as if it had changed hands. Now there were no rebels, but thousands of friendly government soldiers, all looking pleased knowing that now they weren't going to be ordered to attack their present location. They all knew if that had been the case a large majority of them would have been killed. John and Chris were now being approached by someone they guessed must be a Coronel, while Maria had gone over to where Kapia was still sitting.

'You must be John Stone, and Chris Jones, I've been hearing at lot about you two this morning. My country owes you a debt of gratitude for what you've done. But please, if you could just clear up something for me I would be very grateful; it's just that my Intel informs me that you're just a couple of Journalists, well, I know that can't be right...'

'That's right, Coronel, we are just a couple of journalists, but you'd be surprised what just a couple of Journalists with a little bit of imagination can do, sir.'

'So it would seems,' the Coronel said, smiling.

'Well, it's been nice meeting you, sir, oh, my friend Chris here has the coordinates to a location where you'll find around fifty workers that were being held here, I think they'll be pleased to see you, sir.'

'Oh, right, well, I'll get right on it, and thank you again.'

John and Chris then joined Maria and Kapia. Kapia stood and approached John. 'I want to thank you for everything, John, and you, Chris.

'There's no need, Kapia, after all, it was you who killed Joseph Kabila.' John always knew it had to be here. 'So, what now, Kapia, where will you go, and what will you do now that you have your son back?'

Kapia looks at Maria. 'Well, Maria has invited me to stay with her, and I've decided that's what I want to do, at least for now anyhow.'

Maria's smile was full of happiness.

Chris then headed towards the nice cabin, though while not expecting to see too much at all. He was sure that Dubois would have fled, he knew the type of person he was. He soon realised he had fled, but it didn't matter, he knew their paths would cross again, and when they did he knew he would kill him once and for all.

'Well, Chris and I would be more than happy to fly you back to the farm, if that's what you'd like.' John was joking.

'No, no, no, not me, I'm never going in that flying egg again, thank you very much,' Maria insists.

For the next fifteen to twenty minutes they laughed and joked, while talking about their accomplishments.

'John, you're here, I knew you'd come for me.' Martina said, just before two soldiers grabbed her. Tell them, John, tell them to let me go, tell them you're only here because of me.'

John, just nodded at the soldiers and indicating they should take her away.

'But John, why, you know you don't want this,' she said, while being dragged away.

'We'll, she seemed a little sure of herself, John,' Chris said.

'Didn't she just, pal. Didn't she just.

*

John had returned to Maria's farm along with Kapia and her son. Chris had hitched a lift in one of the Chinooks, which had taken him back to Kisangani. From there he'd flown back to London.

John, Maria, and Kapia as well as her son, had also gotten a ride home in one of the Chinooks, which Maria did enjoy. Maria's family had joined them as soon as they'd heard the news, and Gia had smiled at John for the next two days. Maria and

The Journalists - Congo Rescue

John had said their goodbyes and John had been impressed at how well Maria had dealt with it. But now John was in Goma, he was there to pick up his vehicle and to complete his assignment, but before he visited the hospital, he took a little detour to the Brazilian Embassy.

He pulled up outside the gate before exiting his vehicle. The young soldiers that had taken him there from the Goma Residence recognised him instantly, and because of that opened the gate and let him pass. 'Good, Morning, Sir.'

'Yes, good morning to you too,' he said.

The same young soldier then even opened the large mahogany doors that led into the Consular's office, and there he was, sitting at his desk, now looking a little pale after seeing John approaching him.

'Now look, John, I was under orders. There was nothing I could do, it was my president. He ordered me to do it.'

'And your own men, were they part of this scheme you and your so call president cooked up?'

'No John, it's just how it was, they were here already, who else was I going to use.'

John pulled out his pistol complete with silencer and pointed it at the consular's head. 'People like you make my stomach churn, being a consular official doesn't give you the right to use people, especially knowing there's a good chance they're going die. Only god can decide whether we live or die, and apparently he's decided you should die now.'

The consular was about to yell out, but it was too late, John had shot him between the eyes.

'Well, that was quick, sir.'

'Yes, it was just a short visit, that's all.'

'Well, you're welcome to visit anytime, sir.'

'Thank you, that's very kind of you.'

The young soldiers then gave him a salute, and John returned the favour.

*

Finally, John had visited the hospital and completed his assignment. It wasn't pleasant, and he'd decided if his agency gives him an option next time he'd choose the latter, wherever that might be. Now he was back in Kinshasa and at the airport, even though his flight wasn't due for some time. He'd arranged to meet his good friend Harry there, and could now see him approaching.

'Please take a seat, Harry, it's so good to see you again.'

Harry lifted his hat. 'You, too, John. So, you've done it again, I'm so proud of you guys.'

The Journalists - Congo Rescue

'Thanks Harry, but to be honest I'm not sure if we would have managed if not for you.'

'Don't be silly, I just helped with some transport issues, that's all.' Harry said, though appreciating his gesture.

'True, but without that transport, especially the helicopter, well, like I say I don't think we could have pulled it off. So, how much do I owe you, pal?'

'Oh, don't concern yourself, John, besides, now I can do business in the Shaba Province without having to concern myself about that monster Kabila.'

'Oh, Harry, I was just wondering how that deal went, you know the one involving the spears from way back then. I'm guessing you made a fortune.'

'Nah, they were fake, John, it happens in my line of work.'

'Well, that is a shame, Harry. I also seem to remember you saying you know people who deal in uncut diamonds.'

'Yes, that's right and maybe now I'll get some calls from the Shaba province, you never know, hey, John.'

'I doubt it, Harry, not for a while at least, we blew up the mines, and I'm guessing it'll take a while before they're up and running. But don't worry pal, because I kept these for you.' John then gave him a small cloth bag, full to the brim with uncut diamonds.

'Wow, John, there must be a small fortune here, thank you.'

'You're more than welcome, Harry.'

*

John had been delighted to see Harry's face after he'd given him the diamonds. Maria's too, after he'd given her some, he'd known her starting up her farm again was going to mean her having to purchase new equipment after her old equipment hadn't been maintained, thanks to Kabila and his rebels. Chris had given his share to Kapia, he'd felt she deserved it after killing Joseph Kabila, as for her son, well, he'd already had his share, as did the other nine workers that had helped them blow up the minds. It was they who'd told John and Chris where they were hidden. It had indeed been a fantastic day.

*

John was now sitting at his desk when Jonathan approached with a curious look on his face. 'John, am I correct in thinking you said you visited the Brazilian Embassy in Goma?'

'Yes, it was them who asked me to rescue the group, why.'

'Oh, nothing, it's just that the consular there was found dead, the reports suggest he killed himself, the gun was found still in his hand, apparently.'

'Really, that is a shock. Speaking of embassies, Jonathan, my name keeps popping whenever there is an emergency or someone needs rescuing, is there something I can do about that?'

'Yes, I'm sure there is, John, but the real question is, do you want to do something.'

'Um, that is a good point, Jonathan.'

Printed in Great Britain
by Amazon